Netti Barn

THE MENACE

--- PULLING THREADS ---

Book Two

SHERYLL O'BRIEN

This is a work of fiction. All characters in this book are the product of an overactive imagination. Any businesses, organizations, places, events, and incidents are used fictionally. Any resemblance to a real person, living or dead, is a tremendous coincidence.

ISBN 978-1-939351-02-9

WOODWIND PRESS

Printed in United States of America

Mom,

I appreciate how hard you always worked ---

I am amazed at how unaware I was about
how hard you always worked.

ACKNOWLEDGMENT

To my daughters, Hannah and Jessica, thank you for _____. Since neither of you pay much attention to what I have to say anymore, just go ahead and fill in the blank any way you choose.

In all sincerity, I hope you listen to these words – my greatest joys in life begin and end with you.

A heartfelt thank you to my team:

Andria Flores ~ Editor extraordinaire.
Nancy Pendleton ~ Goddess of the publishing world.
Jessica Champion ~ Web designer and manager.
25 Hours Consulting
Daryl Bruinsma ~ Cover Design & Animation.

Testimonials

"One book will set the hook!" ~ Nancy Pendleton

"This avid reader predicts that Sheryll O'Brien will become your favorite author. She's mine." ~ Ruth S. Bodreau

"The characters draw you in immediately. You will worry, laugh, hope, and love right along with them." ~ Donna Eaton

"There is nothing sweeter than a Sunday morning coffee, a blanket, overcast skies, and a *Pulling Threads* novel." ~ Andria Flores

"Everything you'd want in a good book. Humor, romance, suspense and great characters! It even takes place by the ocean! Loved it." ~ Helena Green

"I could write a book about the wonderfulness of it all." ~ Faith

"Hunks, humor, and heartache! What more could you ask for?" ~ Marjorie McCarthy

"*Bullet Bungalow* is a page turning family saga and then *Netti Barn* and *Cutters Cove* come along and add a whole lot of trauma to the drama." ~ Jessica O'Brien

"The most promising new author I've encountered in my publishing career!" ~ Jim P. - Woodwind Press

--- Pulling Threads ---

Bullet Bungalow
Netti Barn
Cutters Cove
They Run
They Hide
They Choose

Coming soon…

PENOBSCOT BAY
A Rocco Fiancetti Incorporated Investigation

Reasons
Rescues
Resolutions
Torment
Tango
Tests
Resolve
Revenge
Rebound

--- Twisted Threads ---

Coming soon…

Her Scream
Stay Safe

Where are you?
August

John Maxwell was passed out cold. His inert body slumped in a seat in the first-class section of a plane, "traveling at some godforsaken Mach-speed across the Atlantic Ocean." Those choice words were uttered during the last seconds of his lucidity. Unfortunately for John, and for his fellow passengers, this was the second trip, "across the fucking pond," he'd made in a handful of days. Despite his aversion to flying, on the first of every August he boards a plane, lashes himself to his seat, and sets about taking the edge off with as many whiskeys as allowed during flight time. When he's sufficiently liquored up, he suggests to everyone within listening distance, to not wake him, "should this fucking plane begin hurtling toward Earth."

John hadn't expected to be returning stateside so soon, in fact, he planned on putting at least 30 days between the torture trips, but there was no reason for him to stay in Madrid— without her.

Where are you?

His heavily encrypted message went unanswered each of the dozen times he sent it. After spending five miserable days alone— confirming what he knew the minute he landed—that she wasn't going to meet him in

Madrid, he packed up and booked a flight home, the one he was mercifully sleeping through. John Maxwell was about to find out that mercy sometimes comes with a price.

"Your turn," he nudged, as he tossed the final handful of A-Z alphabet letters onto their bed.

She pulled a piece of paper, and turned it his way. "I pulled M. You wanted M didn't you?"

He nodded.

"If you got it, where would we be going?" She moved across the bed, and settled into his embrace.

"Madrid."

"Why Madrid?"

"Well, I've never been to Spain..." he sang into her fruity-smelling hair.

She laughed that great laugh of hers, "Well, if you promise to sing that to me once every day while we are there, I'll choose Madrid."

He startled awake.

Netti Barn

No hesitation.

The most important thing to know about John Maxwell is that he is a liar. Nearly everything he has said or done during his entire adult life has been based on a lie. Due to circumstances partly out of his control, but mostly caused by him, it is only a matter of time before his dishonesty is revealed. When that happens, the hearts of the people he loves will be broken, and the relationships that matter most to him will be brought to the brink. There will be plenty of hurt to go around, but the person who will suffer most by his duplicity is Kitt Mahoney. The number of lies this man has told that woman could **never** be counted. When the truth is revealed, and the initial shock has worn off, the deceived woman will start pulling at the threaded lies that have come loose, and the tapestry of the life they created will unravel. John knows that when that happens there may be no coming back for him—for them.

Kittridge Anne Mahoney is the mother of John Maxwell's daughters. She is his best friend—his only friend. John recently heard someone describe Kitt as an Evangeline Lilly lookalike, and while he never made the comparison, he agrees that it is dead-on. Kitt has long, wavy, nutty-brown hair, warm acorn-brown eyes, peaches and cream skin, and a killer smile. A natural beauty, Kitt easily catches a man's eye—she caught John's more than two decades ago.

"Are you ever going to talk?" he asked his new neighbor.

"When I've something to say, John Maxwell, I'll say it."

He smirked, "Didn't expect that."

"No? What did you expect?"

"I don't know, but I didn't expect snippy from someone who looks so…"

"So…what….?" she asked, arms crossed, and the toes of one foot tapping a pissed rhythm.

"Sweet."

"Kittridge. Your mother wants you for supper," Grandpa Mahoney called from the porch.

The obedient girl turned toward home, when…

"See ya, Kittridge."

The "sweet" girl turned on her heels, and charged the new boy. "No one calls me Kittridge! EVER!" Within seconds, the old man had the two 12-year-olds by the scruff of their necks, pulling them apart, and surveying for damage. "No blood drawn this time, but son, if I were you, I'd tread softly with this Irish lass. She can land a punch."

John rubbed at his sore chin, "Wish you told me that earlier, sir."

As the chuckling grandfather and the steaming granddaughter headed inside, John called out after his new neighbor, "What should I call you?"

"If you must call me anything, John Maxwell, call me, Kitt," she said without looking back.

John called her Kitt, until they started high school, then he called her, "his steady girl". The "it" couple at Mayflower-Falls Regional High School had everything going for them, including one too many good times in the back seat of a Ford Bronco. The spring of their senior year, John Maxwell and Kitt Mahoney graduated with honors and a newborn daughter named, Annie. They deferred their acceptance to college, remained living next door to one another at their parents' homes, and learned how to take care of a baby. "She needs to be changed." How to share responsibilities. "It's your turn." And how to lean on one another. "I need to pee, so watch her."

When John headed to UMass Amherst, and Kitt headed to Littleton College, a year later than originally planned, they were no longer a couple, simply co-parenting friends. Mostly. During the week, Kitt did the mothering of Annie, and on weekends, John would take their daughter next door to his parents' place. With their pink bundle in tow, the young father would call over his shoulder…"I've got this Kitt, go out, do your own thing, hang out with Maura."

The young mother did that on occasion, but on other occasions—on many other occasions—Kitt went over to the Maxwell's to, hang out, and watch a movie or something, with John. On occasion—on many occasions—John slipped into old habits and into his high school sweetheart. That all ended when he met Joy Ann Watts.

"Move." The directive came from a beautiful, slight woman with cropped blonde hair and piercing blue eyes standing next to the computer terminal occupied by John Maxwell. He smirked, then went about ignoring her. She grabbed hold of his chair, spun it, and when his legs were facing in her direction, she sat down onto his lap. "This is my seat. If you aren't getting up, then you'll have me on top of you for the next ninety minutes." She readjusted herself against his erection and laughed, "And I don't intend on having to deal with that." Her smile was playful, her intensity was not.

He smirked again, "That will last at least ninety minutes. So, deal."

"Joy."

"What?"

"Joy, my name is Joy."

"We'll see," he smirked.

Joy and John spent their senior year in an all-consuming relationship. "I need to get to class," she said as she rolled from his embrace.

"**We** need to get to class," he corrected.

"Oh, please. You're a Boy Genius, you don't need to do a damned thing for the rest of the year, and you'll still walk away with the highest graduating honors in the CICS department."

"And you'll walk away with second honors, so bring that sweet ass of yours back to this bed."

"If you ravage me one more time, John Maxwell, I won't be **walking** away with anything."

When the couple left for winter break, they were secure in their relationship. They spent Christmas week in Mayflower, John's hometown, and were with Annie and Kitt nearly every minute of that time. It was sort of a trial run, to see how they all got along—they all got along really well. When John and Joy headed back to UMass, they started planning for a future. They never could have imagined what their future would hold—or that it would start the minute they stepped back onto campus. Companies from all over the country began dangling job offers, incredible offers with big sign-on bonuses for each of them. One offer was for the two of them to work together, and it was the most intriguing offer by far. They knew that if they didn't take it, they would be going their separate ways. They took it, and they still went their separate ways.

"I'm pregnant, and I'm not having the baby," Joy told John graduation morning.

"Yes, Joy, you are."

"You can't force me to have a baby, John."

"It's because of the job, right? You'd rather have the job than the baby."

There was not one second of hesitation in Joy's answer. "Yes."

The gutted young man wished there had been hesitation. No matter the number of times he's replayed that conversation—and he has replayed it countless times over the years—he wished that there had been hesitation on her part. Joy's response hurt him deeply, so John did what immature men do, he hurt her deeply. "You don't get the job, Joy, if I don't take the job. I'm the veritable computer genius. They want me. They'll take you as part of the package."

On graduation day, John broke up with Joy, blew up his future, got his degree, went home to Mayflower, got drunk on tequila, and got Kitt pregnant—for the second time. Then he got his head on straight. He could have saved a whole lot of people a whole lot of trouble if he'd gotten a few condoms on straight. Would have. Could have. Should have.

"Dad. Earth to Dad!"

John is pulled back to the here and now by his 14-year-old daughters, Callie, and Tess. He looks into his rearview mirror at his girls, "Did I miss something?"

"We have practice after school, don't forget," they say in unison. They say everything in unison. Though born to different mothers, the doppelganger teens are near-identical. They have long, wavy, honey-blonde hair and vivid blue eyes. Callie's have a tad more aqua in hers, and Tess has a tiny dimple under her left eye. That's what Kitt says, though no one else tends to notice it. John notices it, but since the little dent came from her mother, and nobody in the Mahoney-Maxwell clan ever mentions Joy, he never wades in to the "dimple debate".

The chauffeuring father pulls his BMW SUV to the curb in front of Mayflower-Falls Regional High School. He checks his dashboard clock, though he needn't—it is precisely 7:25 AM. During the school year, Monday through Friday, states within the Eastern Standard Time zone can set their clocks to John Maxwell's arrival at this high school. His life of precision, punctuality, and organization is a direct result of his life choices, as is the fallout he expects any day now.

Ordinary heroes.

"Do you want any help?" John asks from across the kitchen at Bullet Bungalow, knowing full well what Kitt's answer is going to be.

"You can help by staying out of the way, John."

He smirks, then he sets about staying out of the way. From the doorway between the kitchen and living room, he watches Kitt toss an enormous salad, grab it and a tray of burgers and dogs, and hobble out the back door with a, "Help yourself to food and drink," called over her shoulder.

John surveys the array of food and drink options. He takes a pass, but only because he couldn't begin to choose. Every inch of space in the kitchen is covered with enough snack foods and appetizers to feed a small army. That's appropriate, since Kitt's "Army of Ordinary Heroes" is on the way. The most celebrated of the expected guests is David Cluster, a Littleton College campus police sergeant, who is recently out of rehab and coming to Bullet Bungalow. Cluster, as he is affectionately called, thinks he was invited to a small gathering of friends and family. He was, but the festivities have mushroomed into a mammoth party—as most of Kitt's gatherings are wont to do.

Ambushed at the Littleton College Homecoming Dinner Dance by Charles Eaton Alden, Cluster took a single bullet through his spleen and nearly bled out on a beautifully decorated garden terrace at Eaton Hall. Shortly before the festivities began, Mayflower-Falls police detectives, who had been playing Hide 'n Seek with Alden learned why they were playing Hide 'n Seek with Alden—the stalker-turned-attacker-turned-shooter was a bit miffed that Kitt Mahoney was the "in perpetuity" owner of 22 Tarrington Way; a two-acre parcel of land that Alden believed was rightfully his. Legally speaking, Charlie might not have been wrong about that, but legalities tend to get overlooked when one is dealing with someone who's batshit crazy.

Charles Eaton Alden was the great-great-grandson of Alexander Eaton, a wealthy industrialist who crashed headfirst into a speeding bullet after the stock market crashed in 1929. Shortly before his death, Alexander learned that he was the baby-daddy of a boy born to, Sonja Frederickson, an impoverished young woman who gave away the only thing of value that she had—her virginity. Before you could say, "Wham, bam, thank you, Sonja," she was pregnant, and Alexander was on the dole for a few monthly pittance bucks for his kid. In rapid succession, Alexander lost his riches, his reason for living, and he ended it all—without legally claiming his son, or reversing a temporary land deed he made with Patrick and Maria Mahoney, two servants working in the Eaton estate.

Alden learned about this sordid mess, and came to believe that his misfortunes were inextricably linked to the beachfront land grab made by the Mahoney family. It was all downhill from there. Charlie became singularly focused on getting his family's land, and he was willing to go to great lengths to accomplish that goal. A stipulation in the original deed made that a possibility **if** Kitt Mahoney put the land at 22 Tarrington Way up for sale. The crafty, albeit crazy, Alden made a plan to stalk and terrorize the Mahoney women into selling the Laurel Falls property.

"Have fun at Nana Maxwell's party," the stalker said as he emerged from the tree line. He turned the key and entered the bungalow ready to install video cameras in the kitchen and living room, and in the mini and master suites. He made quick work in three of the rooms, but took his time moving through *her* master bedroom. He opened drawers, and ran his fingers along silky pieces folded neatly inside. He lifted a fuzzy sweater from within, and held it to his nose. He breathed in the lingering sweet scent of her, tucked the pink garment back where it belonged, and moved on. He ran his hand along the bed as he made his way to a bank of windows that face *his* ocean. He was eager to enact his plan against the woman who lived there, but he liked the waiting and the watching. It was his foreplay. And like most red-blooded men, he responded to foreplay. Sort of. Thoughts of what was going to happen in that bedroom caused a stirring down below. He loved it. Stroked it.

Before leaving the bungalow, he tossed flowers he ripped from her window box onto the kitchen floor, ground them beneath his boot. He took a final minute on the porch sofa listening to gentle waves roll in. He was enjoying the moment, until his eyes scanned the full of the porch. His erection softened and faded away when he saw **it**, the driftwood sign hanging on the wall by the back door: **Bullet Bungalow**. "Fucking bitch," he snarled as he left the porch and stepped into the tree line along the driveway.

When Detectives Serpico and Phelps figured a few things out, Alden's plan turned to shit. That's when the lunatic gave up on owning 22 Tarrington Way, and settled on a murder-suicide plan. "They know everything about me. They probably figured out why I'm after Kitt Mahoney. Fucking bitch! Fucking cops! I'll never have what is rightfully mine—sure the fuck won't be sitting on the beach at 22 Tarrington Way, anytime soon. Fuck, I'll probably be dead in the next few hours—well, ditto for you, bitch!" A few hours later, the intended suicide victim kidnapped the intended murder victim from a lovely event being held at Eaton Hall and brought her to Bullet Bungalow for their date with destiny. That date would end **very** badly—for Charles Eaton Alden.

John Maxwell wasn't at the Dinner Dance that evening. He spent most of that night at Netti Barn, his software design company, catching up on some work. That's the lie he told everyone. The truth: he was watching over Callie and Tess since Alden was still on the loose, he was monitoring his property for signs of Joy, and he was covering his tracks on a "breaking and entering" thing he did during the hunt for Charles Eaton Alden. Several hours before MFPD Detectives Serpico and Phelps received their legally authorized search warrant for Alden's place, John Maxwell was in the stalker's lair killing the feed to two bedroom-trained surveillance cameras the creep had setup inside Bullet Bungalow. When John was satisfied that he had sufficiently covered his B&E tracks, and that Joy was going to be a no-show that night, he hit the hay. He had just fallen asleep when Detective Serpico, Kitt's very significant other, called.

"Kittridge and Annie are at Mayflower-Falls Regional. There was an incident that started at the college and ended at the bungalow. Alden is dead. Kittridge killed him. Cluster is fighting for his life."

"Are Kitt and Annie injured?"

"Annie's physical injuries are mostly reinjuries from her previous attack by Alden, but she's a wreck emotionally. She was in the thick of it when Alden kidnapped Kittridge, and she and Marcus Fletcher barely missed being shot in the confusion. Kittridge is pretty banged up: concussion, shoulder injury, and a foot that was sliced to the bone, and stitched back together. So far, she hasn't said a word about the shooting or acknowledged that she killed Alden. If you hadn't told me about her Grandpa's gun, John, Kittridge would be dead."

"I'm on my way."

"Your call, but Kittridge is concerned about Callie and Tess seeing all of this. Cluster is touch and go, and the place is locked in a vigil for him."

After tossing and turning for hours that felt like days, John and his younger daughters joined Kitt and Annie, and dozens of others at the hospital to stand in hope for Cluster. Those who attended the Dinner Dance said Alden stepped out from the tree line, shot the Sergeant, and grabbed Kitt. With a gun pressed to her head he spewed his lunacy, and after terrorizing the dining and dancing crowd, he kidnapped Kitt. In an act of heroics that few ever see, Kittridge Anne Mahoney killed her would-be-killer.

"*You fucking bitch!*"

She listened to Alden storm through the room and bang himself against the home office door. *He's going to shoot out the lock!* She dropped behind the desk and waited. As soon as the madman's shot rang out and she heard the sound of the door being kicked aside, she jumped up and fired her grandpa's gun. Twice. Alden stumbled back, his shoulder banged against the doorjamb, causing him to twist. When he fell, he landed on his side. Kitt ducked back down behind the desk and listened to a man moan himself to death.

A month later, Kitt is inducting Littleton College, Sergeant David Cluster, MFPD detectives, Fred Serpico and Steve Phelps, MFPD officers, Michael Monopoli and Grant Speil, Nurse Practitioner, Maura Putnam, a carpenter named Jeff Sanchez, and an alum named Marcus Fletcher, into Kitt's "Army of Ordinary Heroes". They are willing recipients of the honor being bestowed, but they all know what everyone knows—Kitt Mahoney is the real hero.

Glad you think so.

Cluster arrives to a thunderous roar. Chants of, "Cluster! Cluster! Cluster!" ring out, followed by a prolonged hoot and holler display of affection and appreciation. A normally big bear of a man, the sergeant looks like a fraction of himself. Nurse Putnam, said that his stint in rehab was mostly due to the effects of massive blood loss. If that's the case, blood weighs about thirty or forty pounds. Jane Harper, a Dixie born, willowy blonde with hazel eyes and sweet Southern drawl holds onto Cluster's hand like they are super-glued together. Cluster and Jane are a new thing. It is unanimously thought that Cluster deserves a new thing.

John moves to the wall of kitchen windows to participate in the celebration the way he's most inclined—from the sidelines. He surveys the lawn, the beach, and the ocean. Though a lifelong resident of the communities of Mayflower and Laurel Falls, John can count on two hands the number of attendees he knows, and the ones he knows most—Annie, Tess, and Callie—are sitting on squat lawn chairs at the shoreline. Always close, the girls have become *thisclose* after the horrors at Homecoming. He smirks at life's testimony, "Shootings and near-death experiences have a way of bonding sisters."

Just beyond the girls, is an impossible to miss red-haired beauty with an abundant zest for life. Maura Putnam, Kitt's best friend since preschool, is the reason David Cluster is alive today. Word around the medical community is that Maura's years of experience, and brute determination, pulled Cluster from the brink of death, and kept him on this side of living. The Jessica Rabbit lookalike is currently wrapped in the arms of Detective Steve Phelps, frolicking in chest-deep ocean water. It is very obvious that the relationship between the nurse and the cop isn't all "fun and games" it is very serious. As is the relationship of Kitt and Fred who are making the rounds, as though they are a married couple. Annie recently told her father that the two have been sharing Kitt's master suite in a very matrimonial way ever since the Alden nightmare.

"Mom and Fred are…"

"Serious," he finished her sentence.

"Yeup." There was an unusual pause. Annie doesn't pause, Annie pushes.

"What?" the father moved the conversation forward.

"Have you any thoughts on that subject?"

"Nope."

"Feelings?"

"Why are we discussing this?"

"We aren't, really," she hip-chucked him. They shared a chuckle.

After a few minutes, John offered, "Fred's a good guy. Your mother deserves a good guy."

"Glad you think so, because I think she's finished."

"Finished what?"

"Falling in love with him."

The daydreaming man is so lost in the mesmerizing sights and sounds of Bullet Bungalow and in his own thoughts that he doesn't hear the intrusion—until it's too late.

"You planning on joining the party?" Fred asks from behind.

John glances over his shoulder, "You shouldn't sneak up on people."

"Especially people packing heat," Fred laughs. "You still packing, by the way?"

John ignores him.

"Gonna have to tell me why you're licensed to carry concealed someday, John. May as well be today."

John ignores him.

The week leading up to the Dinner Dance, Fred was hunting Charles Eaton Alden—hard. Days earlier the psycho had taken a shot at Kitt and Fred while they were on a run.

They stepped into the tree line, and walked hand in hand. "I need to put on my jacket, it's cool out of the sun." A heavy footfall, and the snap of a branch came from behind them, and set Fred into action. He pivoted toward the sound while wrapping his arm around Kitt's waist. He sort of spun and pushed, and they fell hard onto the ground with him partially on top of her. Fred looked up just as a bullet hit the tree next to them. He rolled off of her, pulled up the leg of his sweats, and grabbed his gun from an ankle holster.

"You okay?" the cop asked.

She nodded.

He pulled himself to his feet, moved behind a tree, and put a finger to his lips. He listened. "He's running." He tossed his cell phone to her, "Call 9-1-1. Say there's an officer involved shooting, and the shooter is heading toward Farmington and Westin. He's driving a red Nissan Altima. Stay down, Kittridge."

That incident pushed the investigation to a frenzied pace. Serpico and Phelps received a search warrant and needed to be at Alden's place, so Fred asked John for help. "…another thing, John, I hope you can stay at the bungalow with the girls, at least until we get back—although it will be a late one."

"No problem."

"The thing is, if Alden shows, he'll be armed. There's a loaded .38 in the desk drawer in Kittridge's office. That's the best I can do."

John stepped way out of his tightly controlled box and lifted his pant leg, revealing an ankle holster and gun to the MFPD detective. In that unguarded moment, he not only showed him that he carried concealed—he told him why. "In case Joy ever comes back."

It has been weeks since those words left his mouth. Fred has been riding him for answers ever since. It's just a matter of time before the detective has the answers he wants about John Maxwell—and he learns that Joy is back.

The truth of the matter.

For the record, John Maxwell, is a spy. Actually, John Maxwell, is a software designer who lives on a farm, and works in a barn, in Mayflower, Massachusetts. John's alter-ego, Sam Sawyer is the spy. Joy Ann Watts is also a spy, a super-spy, really. She is in Mayflower, and she has brought a world of trouble with her. She doesn't know it yet, but she's in deep shit because of a lie John told. He had a very good reason for lying, but that isn't going to matter if the super-spies end up dead.

Special Agent Maxwell and Special Agent Watts work for FICA, the Federal Investigative Cyber Agency, an elite hybrid division of the FBI and CIA. After 9/11, the investigative bureau and the intelligence agency were given a mandate—share information. Period. Hybrid groups became offshoots reporting to one or more of the governmental powers—the power base of FICA is the FBI.

John and Joy were recruited out of UMass Amherst to help develop FICA fifteen years ago. Right after winter break, during their senior year, the two computer "brainiacs" were approached on campus by a guy who had been given their names by a CICS professor. The guy asked them to accompany him to a conference room where he got right to the point.

"I'm FICA Director, Roland Gaffney. I've been looking into your backgrounds, and I am here to recruit you. The FBI is building a team of young, ambitious, highly-skilled, computer geeks to develop a cyber intelligence division housed out of the Agency. I want the two of you on my team."

The "young, ambitious, highly-skilled, computer geeks" signed on, and within a week's time they began FBI training. After extensive background checks, they were put through a battery of physical and psychological exams, were required to pass physical fitness tests, learn basic FBI protocol, and be licensed to Carry Concealed Weapons (CCW). That initial set of requirements needed to be met before they arrived at the FBI training base in Quantico, Virginia. That was the easy part. Going all "secret and shit" was the hard part. As soon as they went dark, they had to go silent. They weren't allowed to disclose to anyone that they'd been recruited by the FBI, or reveal anything about their future plans. In other words, they were no longer allowed to tell the truth. A month before graduating from UMass, John told Kitt his very first big lie.

"Right after graduation, I'm heading to the University of Virginia for my Master in CICS."

"You're what? I thought you were staying at UMass for graduate school," Kitt stammered. When her words were met with silence, she pushed.

"John, what the hell is going on? You haven't seen Annie in months, and now you're moving to Virginia!" **More silence. More Pushing.** "Is this about Joy? I hope not, John, because after her last visit, I don't want her anywhere near Annie."

By the end of that month, a bigger pile of shit hit the fan. After Joy's freak out about the baby, and their subsequent graduation day breakup, John called Director Gaffney to withdraw from the training program. The Director had the couple meet him at UMass for another conference room chat. He stressed the importance of them being part of the post-9/11 intelligence world. Then he made it perfectly clear that Joy was in **only if** John was in. The Director acknowledged Joy's mad computer skills, but he was very frank that the Boy Genius was the draw. Even so, Gaffney let John know that there was a second-choice candidate from MIT waiting in the wings, so he had better work out a solution with Joy. As it turned out, the three of them had to work out a solution. As a rule, the FBI does not recruit pregnant women.

"Maxwell, you'll go through regular recruit training when you get to Quantico. Watts, you'll do the classroom work and continue modified physical workouts throughout the summer, or until such time as the medical professionals tell you to stop athletic training, then you'll go into the computer lab. You two decide what happens with the baby."

The expectant couple, the one who had no future ahead of them, planned one anyway. "What if we hadn't been recruited? Would you want the baby?"

"I told you on our first date that I didn't want kids."

"Yeah, but you were all-in with me and I have a kid. Explain."

"You and Kitt are Annie's parents. She would never be my kid, but all of us could have been a family. That was very appealing to me."

"Was."

She nodded. "John, I want FICA. You want the baby. So let's figure out how this is going to work."

"Kitt and I will raise the baby," the words caught both of them by surprise.

"What makes you think Kitt will agree to raise MY child?"

"Because she's Kitt."

"You're taking a lot for granted, John, but I really hope she'll be our baby's mother."

John's next series of lies to Kitt began the minute his meeting with Gaffney, and his "heart to heart" with Joy ended. "I have reconciled with Joy and we are starting the master's program at UVA immediately." Lie. "I'll travel back here to spend time with you and Annie, sort of divide my time between the Baystate and the Old Dominion." Lie. "I know I've been missing in action a bit, but Joy and I need time to work on our relationship, so I can't come home for a while." **Lie**. "I bought the Netti spread for the Mahoney-Maxwell clan." **Half-lie**.

The truth of the matter: John never intended to travel back and forth between Massachusetts and Virginia. There are no weekends off or furlough times at Quantico—when you get there, you stay there. As for working on his relationship with Joy, that was about three things: their commitment to becoming FBI agents; Joy preparing to deliver their baby; John getting custody of their baby. As for the Netti property, FICA bought Netti Barn as its off-site cyber spy location—John bought the land and the farmhouse courtesy of a big ass FBI sign-on bonus.

When that first round of logistical lies was over, John Maxwell began living his life of deceit as FBI undercover agent, Sam Sawyer. His job at FICA is cyber defense—he protects governmental intelligence assets. Joy Ann Watts began living her life of deceit as FBI undercover agent, Fee Peterson. Joy's job at FICA is cyber offense—she goes after foreign governmental intelligence assets, and anything else she can get her hands on. John is one of the most covert agents at the FBI. Everything he does on behalf of the government leads back to his undercover name. There are five people at the Agency who can link Sam Sawyer to John Maxwell. As for Joy Ann Watts, she is buried so deep in the organization that she no longer exists on paper. FICA refers to her as DOA, an acronym for Dead On Assignment. After fifteen years of undercover work, the spies' identities are at risk, and their lives are at stake. If Joy Ann Watts and John Maxwell don't figure out who the cybermenace known as Hector is, then there is a very good chance that they will both end up D.O.A. Dead On Arrival.

Joy has been off the grid from FICA since August, it is now the end of September. For weeks, John has known that she is in Mayflower. When she was a no-show in Madrid, he returned home to find out why she bailed on their annual sunning and sexing reunion. By the beginning of September, he knew the answers to both of those questions. She went off the grid because of Hector—she was in Mayflower because of him.

"Northeast corner root cellar. If you ever need a last resort."

John offered Joy the last resort years ago. Tonight is the night she will use it.

Stay off the bench.

Special Agent Watts lurks in the shadows. She knows that Special Agent Maxwell has every inch of the Netti property under surveillance. She isn't worried about him seeing her; she's worried that others might have access to the captured images around the farmhouse and barn. That's why she's stayed tucked into the tree line that runs along John's property watching him and the girls. She's been in Mayflower since September 1, incrementally putting herself out in the open. The super-spy wanted him to know she was close by and that she was alive, but now she wants something more. Joy Ann Watts will venture out of the trees, and onto John Maxwell's property, because she is running out of time.

As inconsequential as a breeze, Joy moves toward the root cellar door and pauses. She runs her options through her head one last time, confirming whether this really is a last resort situation. It is. Joy is in Mayflower because it is a matter of life and death, hers and his. She nods her acceptance of the situation, of the plan of action, and sets her course. She enters the cellar. Once behind closed doors, she pulls a tiny penlight from her vest and casts the light around. She scans the dark, dank space, and out of the corner of her eye she notices a tiny speck of white along a door casing, she pulls a piece of paper.

**Stay off the bench,
contact me when you want to come in.**

Joy exhales softly. "He knows I'm in Mayflower. He will help." She folds the paper and tucks it back into the casing; her way of letting him know that she found it. As her hand lowers from the casing toward the doorknob, she notices its shake, accepts that she can no longer still her nerves. The stress of being on the move, and away from her protective lair, is taking its toll. The Special Agent counsels herself, "You need rest—safe rest. Otherwise, you'll make mistakes. Big mistakes. Deadly mistakes. Tomorrow. You come in tomorrow," she whispers. The spy leaves the last resort as quickly and as quietly as a breeze.

Down on Main Street
John managed to put his distractions aside and enjoy Cluster's party for a few hours. It was in full-swing and destined to be an all-nighter when he headed out shortly before ten. Taking the long way home, John travels the length of Main Street past Mayflower Care Center. A lone light shines from a window in the old, brick building. John knows that Joy is near that light. He can feel it. He's always been able to feel her. He relaxes knowing she's safe for the night.

Joy Ann Watts has been staying at the Care Center since Friday. That morning, she was approached by a woman who looked as though she stepped out of the 1960s. The surprisingly young hippy-dippy-do-goody woman with long, gray braided hair, and wearing long, gauzy clothes, approached the "homeless woman" sitting on the bench across from Mayflower-Falls Regional High School. John watched the encounter.

"May I sit?"
Joy nodded ever so slightly.
"The building I walk to every morning is a homeless shelter in case you need a place to stay or a hot meal." She reached into her satchel and pulled out a brown paper bag. Without another word, the hippy-dippy-do-goody woman placed the bag on the bench, got up and walked to the corner.

Joy opened the bag and removed a plastic-wrapped sandwich, a bottle of water, and an apple. She watched the woman walk three blocks north and enter a brick building. "A homeless shelter. That could work." Joy ate her sandwich, spent a few more hours on the bench, then went to the Mayflower Care Center.

She has been staying there ever since. John exhales a sigh of relief, then offers a professional observation, "It's time to come in, Special Agent Watts."

Bullet Bungalow

Fred brings in the last of the party stuff from outside—Kitt tosses him a dishtowel.

"I'd say that was a success," she offers one of her million-watt smiles.

Silence.

"Cluster looks really good, considering…"

Silence.

"I think Maura might be pregnant…"

Silence.

"Fred Chester Serpico!" She sends a handful of soapy water his way.

"What!?"

"Did you hear a single thing I just said? Apparently, you did not because I said that Maura might be pregnant."

"For real?"

"No! I was trying to get your attention."

"Well you got it."

He wipes himself with the towel, then nestles close behind Kitt. The man casually excites – the detective casually examines. "John seems a bit off. Distracted. Is everything okay with him?" A little touch. A little nibble.

"Hmmmm, this is very okay, Fred."

The detective tries again, "I don't know John really well, but..." A little touch. A little nibble.

"But? What? Fred?" Kitt demands.

"You tell me. You're the one who knows him."

Kitt twists in the detective's arms, and wraps her dishpan hands around his neck, "Give."

"Only if you swear not to repeat a single word…" he pauses for emphasis, "I mean it, not to Maura, Steve, Annie, Cluster, Jane, and especially not to John. I mean it Kittridge."

She doesn't have a problem keeping secrets from the others, but keeping secrets from John—that's different. "You're asking a lot, Fred. John and I don't keep secrets from each other. That's why our relationship works."

The detective is adamant. "I won't tell you anything unless you swear secrecy from John."

"Alright, alright."

"John wears an ankle holster and carries a concealed weapon."

"John. The computer geek. That, John? He carries a gun? For what? Troubleshooting?" Kitt laughs big.

Fred does not laugh.

Carrying concealed.

John drops off Tess and Callie in front of the high school at precisely 7:25 Monday morning. As he pulls away from the curb, a homeless woman steps forward and gently bumps against the front of his SUV. She steps back onto the curb and waves the driver on. "Move, move, you're in my way."

When the Special Agent gets to the farmhouse, he gives the SUV a once over finding what he knew he'd find. He pulls Joy's note and a tiny magnet out from under the right front panel of the SUV. The note reads: **root cellar, midnight.** "I have a lot to do before midnight." He begins by opening Netti Barn for Greg and Matt, two MIT interns that he has working for him. Netti Barn isn't your run of the mill software design company, it's a FICA spy location, *and* it is the central part of John Maxwell's cover. The Special Agent puts a concerted effort in bringing legitimacy to his company—while securing the covert defense center. Achieving the correct balance between those two objectives is why John doesn't have "employees" underfoot. Each semester, he commissions college students through work study or internship programs, to create software programs for the design company's legitimate customers, of which there are hundreds. The "here today – gone tomorrow" association between John and the students allows for set boundaries, ergo no bonding, no questions. As soon as the business owner sets that day's work expectations, the FICA agent heads to his home office computer center. "Let's see what the fuck Hector's up to."

Down on Main Street

On the bus trip to work, Lynn McAvoy thinks about the new woman who came to the Care Center. Lynn has worked in social services for years, and she knows her clientele. "The new woman isn't homeless. She shows signs of outdoor living, with a layer of dirt here and there, but she isn't homeless," Lynn whispers to the side window that holds her reflection. "I don't know why the woman is hiding, or from whom, but it doesn't really matter. She's got a safe place at the Care Center."

MFPD

At the Mayflower-Falls Police Department, Detective Steve Phelps is pacing. He always paces when he processes information. Today, his partner, Detective Fred Serpico, dropped a boatload of information that Steve needs to think through. Fred sits back and waits. And waits. And waits some more.

"Okay. Let me see if I have this straight. John Maxwell is licensed to carry concealed.

You found this out the night we were hunting Charles Alden, and you asked John to stay with the girls at Bullet Bungalow. You were concerned that you were leaving him unarmed, so you told him where he could find a loaded .38 in case Alden showed up. He lifted his pant leg and showed you his ankle holster. Then he told you that he carries for protection from Joy, the mother of his daughter, Tess. He also told you that Kitt, the woman he's known forever, the mother of two of his kids, and pseudo-mom to his third kid, has no idea John packs heat. Do I have this right so far?"

Fred clears up one point, "John said he carries in case Joy ever comes back."

Steve nods. "Right. Now, since the time you found out about John carrying concealed, you've prodded him into telling you specifically why he carries. He has balked at or ignored your attempts. This doesn't sit well with you, so you've gone digging into John's personal life— like any respectable detective would do." Steve stops pacing and looks Fred in the eye, "I have a question."

"Shoot."

"Are you out of your fucking mind?"

Fred chuckles, "I have a question. Actually, I have two."

"Shoot."

"Since Alden was the immediate threat that night, why didn't John say he was carrying a weapon in case Alden showed up? Why did John mention Joy, a woman he hasn't seen in fourteen years?"

Steve starts pacing. Again.

Netti

Under the darkness of a near starless sky, Joy enters the root cellar. She finds it empty. She turns to leave when the sound of a vibrating cell phone pulls her attention toward the far-right corner. She grabs the cell and reads the text: **If you haven't been followed, I'll text back in five minutes. Then come in.** John spends the time he should be watching his security cameras thinking about the weirdness of Joy Ann Watts and John Maxwell.

While waiting for the birth of their baby, the spies created an alphabetical list of cities across the globe where they planned to meet every August. The month-long hiatus was a request they made—a condition they set—when their boss gave them their permanent assignments.

"A month," **Gaffney repeated,** "for both of you?"

"Yes," **John answered.**

"Simultaneously?"

"Yes!" **Joy's response neared the line of unacceptability. She pulled back on her tone, but not on her conviction.** "Given the assignment you gave me, it is little to ask, Director."

Gaffney nodded in her direction, "Agreed. But, having the two of you gone at the same time could be problematic."

"We are working on a list..."

"An alphabetical list..."

"Of cities that we plan on visiting each August..."

"We will give you that list, so you will know where we'll be..."

"My assignment requires 24/7 commitment, Director. I figure I'm going to need August—with John."

"Submit your list before you begin your assignment. No one else is to see it, know about it, or have a copy of it."

"Yes, sir," they replied and complied.

The process of choosing their destination cities was very low-tech. They threw A-Z labeled pieces of paper onto their bed, took turns pulling a letter, and then naming their world city. "Genoa," John said.

Joy laughed. "You're kidding, right?"

"No."

"What is it with you and Italy? You chose Florence, already. Not only is that an Italian city, but F alphabetically precedes G. That means we'll be in Italy two years in a row."

He shrugged, "So?"

"Maybe we should change the rules of this game."

"First, this isn't a game, and second, there are no rules." John pulled Joy beneath him, putting the non-game-game on hold, and setting a few sexual rules. "I'm in control, Joy. Don't move. Don't touch. Don't talk."

She did as she was told—until she just couldn't anymore, "John," the quiet call announced the beginning of her orgasm, "John," the almost painful whimper announced its end.

"Joy," he groaned with his release. When his strength returned, he got onto his elbows, lifting just far enough to take his weight off of her expanded belly. He ran his fingers through her cropped hair, and let himself get lost in her piercing blues—until he just couldn't anymore, "Joy…"

"Don't, John. Please, don't."

He rolled off. She rolled away.

After a shower, dinner prep, and dining, the two got back to their project. The one that would reunite them each year.

"Ica! I was hoping I would get the letter I," she squealed.

"Ica? Why Ica," he asked, his trademark smirk present and accounted for.

"I want to see the nearby Huacachina."

"Explain."

"Huacachina is a village that was built around a desert lake. Legend has it that a beautiful princess stopped at a small lagoon to bathe. She was startled away from the tiny pool by an approaching hunter. In her haste to leave, she dropped her hand mirror into the water—the mirror turned the tiny lagoon into a magnificent lake. As the princess ran away, the folds of her long cloak streamed behind her, creating ribbon-like sand dunes. I've seen Huacachina online. It's hard to imagine that it is real – a city surrounding a beautiful lake in the middle of a desert. It pushes against what you think is possible. The villagers of Huacachina still tell the story of that oasis princess. She is rumored to live in the lake of Huacachina as a mermaid."

"Put it on the list," he encouraged.

The Special Agents followed that list faithfully, meeting in the city assigned to that year and that letter. Year one, Athens. Year two, Berlin. Year three, Calgary. And so on. The alphabetical reunions began when, their daughter, Tess, turned one and thirteen years in, they were scheduled to meet in Madrid this past August. The minute John landed in Spain; he knew Joy wouldn't show. He could feel it.

Where are you?

His heavily encrypted message went unanswered. He waited a handful of days, left Madrid, returned to Mayflower, holed himself up at Netti Barn, created a new cyber signature, and went hunting the huntress.

John is pulled from his ruminating by the alarm on his cell. He sends Joy an **all-clear** text, and within a matter of seconds she comes through the back door. They stand motionless, staring at one another, for what feels like hours.

"Sorry about Madrid, John."

He motions for her to follow. She moves as quietly as a cat across the room.

"The girls aren't here. You don't have to be quiet."

"They're beautiful, John."

"They're in danger, Joy."

She nods. "You're my last resort," she whispers.

"I know."

Start talking, Mahoney.

Fred can't avoid the nagging questions banging in his head. He gets out of bed, goes to the kitchen, stands in front of a darkened window, and starts processing. "Why was John armed that night? It would make sense that he was carrying because of Alden, but he said he was armed because of Joy. What is it about Joy that John finds threatening? And does he carry all the time? Is Joy a constant threat to him? Is she a threat to Kittridge, and the girls?" Fred tosses back a glass of water, then tosses out a thought, "I'd bet anything that Joy is in Mayflower." The determined detective decides to get some answers. He crawls into bed, moves close to Kitt, and pulls her into his spoon.

"Kittridge."

"Mmm."

"Are you asleep?"

"Mmm."

"I think Joy is in town."

Kitt bolts upright, "I'm awake, now!" She turns on a bedside lamp, gets up onto her knees, and bounces up and down on the bed. "Tell me. Tell me. Oh. My. God. Tell me!"

"You first," Fred says as he leans back against the headboard, and crosses his arms behind his head.

"Me? What am I supposed to tell you? I don't know anything."

"You're the only one who knows about John and Joy. Unless I have a little background, the stuff that I'm thinking won't make sense. So, start talking, Mahoney."

"There really isn't a whole lot to tell. I met Joy Ann Watts midway through John's first semester of his senior year at UMass. They were hot and heavy by the time he brought her to Mayflower. I got the impression that John was testing Joy out. You know, how would Joy deal with me and Annie being part of their lives. I liked Joy, immediately. She was warm and very approachable, but she had an edge too. She challenged John. I liked that about her. She got on very nicely with Annie, and we spent oodles of time with them during Christmas break. We all had a blast together sledding, snowball fights, building snowmen; we even went on a sleigh ride. I was hoping John would end up with Joy. I actually envisioned the three of us blending our families together—if they married and had children."

"Wow, I didn't expect that story based on future events."

"Well, that's only part of the story. Everything went sideways after winter break. John and Joy only came to Mayflower once during the spring semester. I think it was sometime in March when they visited Annie and me. It was an awful visit. The tension between the former lovebirds was almost palpable. The warm, engaging, and open Joy had been replaced by a barely communicative, almost hostile woman. I didn't like new Joy. I certainly didn't like her for Annie, anymore. John and I had words over it. I asked if they were having relationship issues, or if I had done something to offend Joy, or if she was on drugs? Honestly, the change in her was dramatic enough to warrant those questions. I told John I no longer wanted Joy around Annie. I never saw Joy Ann Watts again. John and Joy broke up at their graduation, then reconciled almost immediately. And truth being stranger than fiction, Joy and I ended up pregnant at the same time. John intended to split his time between Massachusetts and Virginia, where Joy had relocated, but he ended up staying there for all of Joy's pregnancy—for all of my pregnancy. When he came home nine months later, he had Tcss with him. Joy gave custody of their beautiful baby girl to John. The rest is history, as they say."

Fred gets out of bed and goes to the darkened bedroom window. Kitt knows he is processing, so she waits patiently for the questions that will eventually come. Okay, she doesn't wait patiently, but she waits.

"What about John?"

"What about him?"

"You said there was tension between John and Joy, and that she was a different person in March."

"She was."

"And John? Was he different, too?"

Kitt gets up and joins Fred at the window. "Now that you mention it, John was different. Not with Annie, although he wasn't seeing her, so that was different, but he was very different with me. He was guarded, or secretive, or maybe vague is a better description."

"Can you give me an example?"

"The University of Virginia," her answer is quick, and direct. "A little background might be helpful. When John and I were in high school and filling out applications for UMass, he was already planning a minimum six year stay at the campus. He **never** said anything about going anywhere else for his master's degree. Then, bam! He calls me one night, after my not seeing or hearing from him in weeks, and tells me he's going to UVA for his Masters in CICS, and that he was leaving right after graduation—which, by the way, was only a month away."

"And Joy relocated to Virginia right after graduation?"

Still looking out the window, Kitt nods.

"Do you think John's secrecy about Virginia was because he was going with Joy and didn't know how to tell you?"

Kitt turns toward her inquisitor, gives his question some thought before answering. "I was going to find out eventually, so why keep Virginia a secret?" Kitt is silent for another couple of minutes, then adds, "When John told me about Virginia, we had already had words about Joy. I was very vocal about my not wanting Joy in Annie's life, so maybe he struggled with telling me about his plans from that perspective." She bangs a few more thoughts, finally settling on one, "I think there was something else going on. I never really pulled the thread on all this, but my gut is saying it was something else."

"Mine, too," the detective says.

We need to talk.

     Lynn McAvoy is concerned. To be more accurate, a gnawing feeling began as soon as she woke that morning, and settled deep during her bus trip into town. Concern pushed hard when she stepped off the bus and saw that the new woman wasn't there. Again. "She's been sitting on that bench for weeks. She's not on the bench. She's not coming to the Center. Did whoever she's hiding from find her? I'll give it a couple days. Then, I'll give Detective Steve a call."

Netti

John is no sooner awake when he sees Fred's F-150 pull onto the driveway, Bob Seger's *Her Strut* blaring from inside the truck. John rushes to meet him at the back door. He is handed a Perks coffee from the uninvited guest—he hands it back, "I've got a full pot on. Why are you here Serpico?"

     Fred smiles. "Didn't know we were on a last name basis, Maxwell." He smiles wider. "Thought we should talk."

     "Some other time," Maxwell tries to shut the door.

     Serpico puts his hand up to stop it, "This is my nice visit, John. The next time I'll come loaded for bear."

     John shuts the door.

Joy stayed in John's room while he dealt with the intrusive detective. She has questions upon his return. "Is that usual, him coming here?" she asks.

"Nope," John sits at the foot of the bed. "First time actually."

"Is he a problem for me? Do you think I should go?" Joy inches down the bed, wraps her arms around his neck, and leans her naked breasts against his back.

"He's a problem for me, Joy. I slipped up when he was working a case and he needed my help. And, yes, you should go, but last resort, remember?"

Joy nods. She kisses John's neck, then nudges his shoulder, "Did you just say that *you* slipped up?" she asks skeptically.

He nods, leans forward and rests his forearms on his thighs. "Serpico asked me to guard Kitt, Annie, and Maura Putnam at Bullet Bungalow while he hunted a lunatic who attacked Annie, stalked Kitt, and used her as a moving target when she was out on a run. The detective didn't want to leave all of us unprotected at Kitt's bungalow, so..."

"So, you showed him that you carry," Joy finishes his sentence.

"Yeup."

She leans forward, and sprawls across his back. As she wraps her arms around him, she peppers little kisses here and there, then she bolts up straight, "Did you call him Serpico?"

He nods.

"Detective Fred Serpico?"

"Yeup."

"The Fred Serpico who was married to Roni Shields?"

He nods.

"Shit!"

"That's what I said when I figured it out." He gets up, kisses Joy long and deep, then heads to Netti Barn. He opens the software design portion of the spy station for the interns, loads them up with projects, and tells them to call, "only if there's an emergency," then heads back to the farmhouse. John stands a minute on the back porch taking in the beauty of his farmland. It strikes him how much he loves this place, and how contented he is with his life. "A life of lies," he scoffs, and heads inside. When he left his bedroom, a little more than a half-hour before, Joy was in his bed. When he returns, she is in his home office.

"Get out," he calmly says, though he is pissed.

"Sure. I'm already done with what I needed to do."

"Stay out of my office, and stay off my systems. I'm only saying it once, Joy." He sits at his computer and keystrokes a bit. "You were checking on Hector."

She pales. "Do you know the whole story of Hector? I mean the one that involves me?"

The spy doesn't answer her question. "Come on Joy, we need to talk." When John Maxwell said they needed to talk, what he really meant is Joy needs to talk—he needs to get information. They head to the kitchen.

Joy sits. He stands.

Joy procrastinates. He waits.

The Special Agent taps her fingers on the kitchen table; it's a nervous habit she developed way back when, and it's one the super-spy hasn't been able to break. The movements are reflexive, they are quick, they do not make the slightest sound. John smirks. She becomes aware that he's watching her fingers—she stops their movements—gets annoyed that she showed her "tell".

Joy pulls a cleansing breath and begins. "Hector is a cybermenace. He has been hacking FBI and DEA systems for years, nearly a decade, really. He uses the information he gathers to warn major drug cartels about planned Federal raids. His warnings give the syndicates time to move their product, money, and weapons. When the Feds execute the raid, they end up with nothing to show for their undercover work. In some of the botched raids, agents, cops, and civilians have died."

John raises his hand, leans back against the counter, and crosses his ankles, "I know what Hector does, and the fallout from Hector's actions, Joy. What I don't know is why you are involved. There are enough Federal drug agents and computer analysts to hunt a cybermenace who's messing up drug raids. You are the preeminent huntress of cyberland. You are the most covert agent in the Federal government. You are listed Dead On Assignment. What you do for our government is highly classified, and you're so deep undercover there isn't even air where you work. So, why are **you** involved with Hector?" he asks pointedly.

Joy gets off her chair, sprints across the kitchen, and hops onto the counter next to John, "About two years ago, my systems showed signs of hacking, just little nuisance stuff at first. Within a few months, my hacker identified himself as Hector. Not only did Hector let me know he was on to the preeminent cyber huntress, he also let me know that he is the 'cyber-drug-savior' the one who'd been tipping off the drug syndicates. When he outed himself as the cybermenace, I reported him to Director Gaffney. I also told the Director that Hector had been hunting me, and getting a little too close for comfort. Gaffney put a dedicated FICA team out to find him. The agents hunted the menace around the clock, and since Hector hunted me around the clock, it meant that the agents hunted me around the clock. It made it difficult to do my work, and created exposure channels.

All of a sudden, the cyber huntress, the ghost of cyberland, was on the radar of a team of agents. Within a matter of days Hector started referring to me as DOA. I don't know what the hell happened, but Hector was 'on' to the most covert agent at FICA. The fact that he used **that** acronym—meant that he knew he was trailing a Dead On Assignment FICA agent. In time, he made the connection between DOA and my undercover FICA name, Fee Peterson. **No one** at FICA, or anywhere else in the world, refers to me as Fee Peterson, anymore. I haven't used that alias, or any other for that matter, for more than a decade, but Hector somehow made the connection. This summer, he started bragging that he finally unmasked the preeminent cyber huntress. He said his next mission was to unmask the mighty Boy Genius, Sam Sawyer.

"Shortly before I was set to go to Madrid, Hector contacted me and challenged me to a game. There was only one objective to his game—I needed to identify him by October 13 or he kills me. My only out, the only way to stay alive, is to tell Hector who Sam Sawyer is, so he can kill you. Hector says you are his nemesis."

John moves in front of Joy so she can't get off the counter. He stares her down—she holds his stare.

"Did Hector ever refer to you as Joy Ann Watts?"

"No."

"But you think he knows your real name?"

"I wasn't sure at the time he challenged me, but I don't think so now. I've been moving around for the past couple of months. Most of that time I've stayed underground, but every so often I put myself out in the open. I've never picked up a tail, or even suspected I had one. To be on the safe side, I stayed away from Madrid."

"Because Director Gaffney has our alphabetical list?"

She nods. "If it wasn't me who messed up two years ago, and Hector learned who I am from someone at FICA, then who's to say he couldn't find out about our yearly reunions and show up in Madrid? If that happened, he'd have me and you."

John spreads Joy's legs and moves between them. He pulls her hips forward, and slides her the length of him until her feet find floor.

She pulls a shaky breath, then another.

He locks onto her piercing blues, "If it comes to me or you, give me up."

THE MENACE

Hector's heart thumped wildly when the cyber huntress came back to cyberland. She'd been off the grid for so long, he thought he'd driven her away for good. "The game. You disappeared right after I challenged you to play the game. Why is that?" His fingers fly across his keyboard, he stares intently at his monitors. He's looking, searching, hunting in the depths of cyberland. "Where are you DOA. Was that deep dive a tease—a signal to me? Are you looking for me OR are you on the run?" He laughs, a bit manically. "You must think I really have unmasked you? Is that why you've been gone? OR did you disappear because you're protecting FICA's preeminent defender, Sam Sawyer? Are you with him? Is that where you've been all this time?"

Hector feels a nipping at the edges of his mind. "I know you want to weigh in on this, Troy, but I DON'T WANT YOU TO!" The cybermaniac starts keystroking—looking for a thread to pull on DOA's recent visit to cyberland. "All I need is a slip up like the one from two years ago. That tiny blip put me onto your trail DOA. Just give me one more thread—I'll pull it and unravel the fucking mystery of who the preeminent huntress and preeminent defender are. Just make one more mistake and I'll have your real name. And when I have it—I will find you—I will torture you—I will break you. And when I do—you will tell me the identity of the Boy Genius behind Sam Sawyer—my Achilles."

Hector can no longer keep **him** from breaking through the madness.

"You'll never find out who Sam Sawyer is, Hector."

"Shut up, Troy!"

Quantico is in Virginia.

Prompted by her trip down memory lane with Fred the night before, Kitt pulls her "John Box" from a shelf in her walk-in closet and takes a seat on the floor. The box holds mementos from her years in high school and college—it is big, and it is full. It contains pictures, party invitations, newspaper clippings, movie ticket stubs, all the things a teenaged girl keeps. Kitt pulls a black stone and gold banded ring from inside. "John's class ring." She smiles as she examines it, "The band is still wrapped with yards of orange yarn, faded yarn," she sighs. She thinks back to the day he gave it to her.

"Give me a T – I – G – E – R – S. Gooooo, Tigers!"

The "it" couple sat in the stands at the Homecoming Weekend football game. It was **the** most important game of the season. The Tigers of Mayflower-Falls Regional High School, were hosting their arch rival team, the Beavers of Beverly-Crossing Regional High School. It was a cool, crisp fall evening, and Kitt was snuggled close to John, wearing his favorite sweatshirt, the one he gave her when he asked her to "go steady". He nudged her thigh with his,

"I want my sweatshirt back," he casually said, his eyes trained on the gridiron.

"What? Why? Are you breaking up with me?" she croaked.

He smirked, "Of course not."

"Then…"

He stood up, reached into his front pocket, and pulled something from inside, "I thought I'd replace it with this."

"Your class ring. You got it?"

"It came this morning. Didn't you get yours?"

"No. Not yet."

He shrugged. "So, Kitt Mahoney, do you want to wear my ring?"

"Yes!"

John slipped it onto her finger, "It's pretty big. Don't lose it."

"Oh, I won't John. I'll wrap it with yarn 'til it fits. Don't worry, I'll take care of it, and keep it forever."

Kitt slips the clunky ring onto her finger, "It still fits." She exhales a lifetime of memories as she takes it off, and drops it into the box. It falls onto a stack of postcards that are tucked into a corner. "John's picture postcards from his business-vacation trips." She quickly flips through them. All dated sometime in August, and each has the standard, **having fun, wish you were here,** message. Kitt looks at the scenic pictures on each card, puts them back into the box, and gives her head a little shake. She doesn't know why, but ever since her conversation with Fred, the postcards have been creeping through her mind. "Huh, I didn't get one from Madrid. I guess that's what's bothering me."

MFPD

Fred fills Steve in on the Kitt-John-Joy college saga. As usual Steve begins pacing. When he finishes processing, he lays out the facts, as he's heard them. "Okay, let me see if I have this straight. John meets Joy. They get hot and heavy. John introduces Joy to Kitt and Annie. Everyone likes one another and plays nice together. John and Joy change over spring semester—she becomes hostile toward Kitt—he becomes vague. John and Joy break up at graduation. John comes home and gets Kitt pregnant. John goes to Virginia and stays there with Joy, who is also pregnant. John comes home with baby, Tess. Kitt delivers baby, Callie. Joy heads for places unknown. John packs heat in case Joy ever comes back. My partner thinks Joy is back. Did I miss anything?"

"No, but I thought of something while you were rambling," Fred digs.

"Recapping," Steve corrects.

"Right, recapping," Fred pauses and looks out the bank of office windows. "Let's assume that John and Joy broke up at graduation **because** she was pregnant. Tess and Callie were born within days of each other, so it's very plausible that's why they broke up. Maybe Joy wanted an abortion, and John wanted her to have the baby, and that caused the breakup. Joy clearly didn't want the baby; she gave custody of Tess to John the minute she gave birth. So why did she have the baby? Why didn't she end her pregnancy?" Fred answers his own question, "Maybe she had religious or pro-life reasons. Or ... I'm generalizing here, Steve, but women who get pregnant and don't want the baby do not go through a pregnancy and then immediately give the baby to the father. They have an abortion, sure. They put the baby up for adoption, sure. But carry a baby for nine months because the baby-daddy wants her to. I don't see it. I think there's some other reason why Joy decided to have the baby."

The detective processes for a few minutes, then gets to the crux of matter. "According to Kittridge, John and Joy changed when they went back to UMass after Christmas break. John went M.I.A.—Joy became hostile— the two of them became secretive. John, the guy who always planned to do his graduate studies at UMass, and the father of Kittridge's daughter, planned the next few years of his life without her knowledge or input. His next few years weren't in Amherst, they were in Virginia. Quantico is in Virginia..."

Steve interrupts, "I really wish you wouldn't go there, Fred."

"I think John and Joy are Feds."

"Damn it all, Fred." Steve starts pacing.

Fred waits until his partner collapses in his chair from the marathon event. He takes a file from his desk drawer, drops it onto his desk, the one with the nameplate that reads **Detective Serpico**. He gives it a good long stare, gives Steve a good long stare, and leaves the office. When he returns an hour later with two Perks black and white coffees, he doesn't find his partner pacing like he is apt to do—he finds him staring out the window like Fred is apt to do. "Well, this can't be good," Fred laughs.

Steve doesn't turn around; he simply addresses Fred over his shoulder. "When you told me your marriage ended because of too many years undercover, I assumed you were the one undercover."

"I know."

"Your wife Veronica is DEA."

"Ex-wife."

"So, Veronica was the one who did the undercover work?"

"Come on Steve, you know I can't confirm or deny anything about an undercover Federal agent, assuming we're even talking about an undercover Federal agent."

Steve scoffs and gives his head a good shake. "So far as I know, Detective Serpico, you aren't supposed to out an undercover Federal agent, either."

"I didn't. It's not my fault that you took a file from **my** desk and read it, Detective Phelps. So far, the only thing I confirmed is that my ex-wife's name is Veronica." Fred laughs big. "I suggest that we move on from this non-discussion, Detective Phelps."

The detectives put in several quiet hours before calling it quits early afternoon. Fred places three phone calls before leaving the MFPD parking lot.

Call #1: "Hey, Kittridge, can you tell John you're gonna get Callie and Tess from basketball practice for another sleepover."

"Sure. Is anything wrong?"

"I need to talk to John."

"Fred..."

"I'll fill you in later, I promise. Keep my bed warm."

Kitt smiles big when she ends the call. She knows what *that* means.

Call #2: "Hey, Roni, I could use some help. Give me a call. The sooner, the better. Thanks."

Call #3: "Hey, John. I'll be at the farmhouse tonight at nine. We have things to discuss."

It's your tell.

DEA Special Agent, Veronica Shields, listens to her ex-husband's voicemail message. Twice.

"**Hey, Roni, I could use some help. Give me a call. The sooner, the better. Thanks … Hey, Roni, I could use some help. Give me a call. The sooner, the better. Thanks.**"

The woman who fears nothing and no one notices the tremble in her hand when she puts her cell onto her desk. "I wish you needed me." She picks up her phone, immediately puts it back, "There was a time when you needed me, and you wanted me. I'm the one who walked away," she angers at herself—for the umpteenth time. She pushes back at her emotions and stiffens her spine. "For God's sake. The ink on the divorce papers of Veronica Shields and Fred Serpico dried a long time ago, Roni. It's time to move on." She pushes from her desk and takes a minute at the window overlooking Puget Sound. A memory finds her headspace.

"Do you mind?"

She looked up, found his eyes, and smiled. She lifted her backpack from the seat next to her, then scanned the room, "I was saving this seat for someone."

He smiled, "No problem. I'll go sit up front."

A wide smile brightened her face. "I was saving it for you. I've been saving it for you for weeks."

"I know." He smiled *that* smile of his. "Fred Serpico," he said, as he sat and stretched his legs out into the aisle.

"I know." She smiled *that* smile of hers. "Veronica Shields," she said, as she ran her fingers through her cropped hair.

"I know." He smiled again. "You're a psych major with a minor in foreign language." He noticed the tiny intake of breath, "Don't worry, I'm not a stalker, I'm just working on my investigative skills..."

"Because you're a psych major with a minor in criminal justice. Don't worry, I'm not a stalker. I'm just working on my investigative skills."

"Yeah? You're going into law enforcement?"

She smiled and shrugged her shoulders. "Not sure where I'll fit in, but yeah."

By first semester, senior year, Veronica Shields knew where she would fit. "I signed up for the DEA seminar. Do you want to come?"

"Nope."

"If I get the DEA..."

"You will. You're a good fit, even without all the languages you speak."

"But..."

"Roni. Go after whatever it is you want."

"And if I want you?"

"You've already got me."

Veronica picks up her cell and returns Fred's call. She braces herself for the sound of his voice. It's her weakness.

"Roni, thanks for calling back."

"No problem, Serp. What do you need?"

"Information on John Maxwell."

There is an almost indiscernible intake of breath followed by, "Don't know who that is, Fred."

"How about Joy Ann Watts?"

Another intake of breath followed by, "Don't know who that is, either."

"Yes, you do, Roni. I heard it in your breath. It's your tell," Fred accuses.

"Let me **tell** you this straight up, Serpico. You don't need to discern anything from my breathing—just listen to my words. Leave whatever you're doing, alone," Veronica ends the call.

Fred got the confirmation he needed. "John Maxwell is a Fed. Joy Ann Watts is a Fed. Roni won't even touch this. God, John, how deep are you?"

Netti

John is waiting outside the farmhouse for, "the pain in the ass" to arrive. When he does, he exits his truck in typical Serpico style.

"What, no invite inside for coffee or tea, maybe a beer, John?"

"Get to it, Fred. I've got things to do," he says impatiently.

The detective leans back against his truck and stares, "How deep undercover are you?"

The undercover agent remains silent.

Fred presses in. "Okay. That ends the question and answer portion of this evening's game of, *Let's Tell the Truth – Or Not.*" Fred steps away from his truck and gets into John's personal space.

He doesn't move. He doesn't flinch. He wants to punch Fred.

"Now for the, *What I Know* portion of this evening's game. When you and Joy went to Virginia, you did not go to UVA. You went somewhere else in Virginia—we'll come back to your destination, in a minute. Interestingly, before you two left Massachusetts, you got your CCW licenses." Fred waits for John's response, he is met with silence. He begins again, "The way this all shakes out is this: you graduated from UMass with a degree in CICS, **and** a license to carry. The woman in your life, at that time, also got a degree in CICS, **and** a license to carry. Now, the other woman in your life, the one you've been involved with, on some level, for two decades, the woman who lived with you at this farmhouse for more than a decade, the woman who is the mother of your daughters was kept in the dark about your weapons, and I suspect a whole lot more."

He waits for a response. He gets none. He continues.

"Now, back to the questions. I don't expect you to answer them, but I'm gonna keep looking for the answers, so consider this your heads up. How did you afford all this," Fred indicates the Netti property, "right out of college? Inheritance? Nope. Your parents and grandparents are still alive. Maybe you got a big fat signing bonus from your new employer? Nope. You didn't have a new employer—you opened your own business—right out of college—with three kids to support."

John really **wants** to punch him.

"Now, for the, *What I Think* part of this evening's game. The Boy Genius and his girlfriend were recruited by the FBI or CIA while at UMass. They trained while still at college, and got their CCW licenses before they graduated. Things went sideways, and the Boy Genius and his girlfriend broke up at graduation. I figure Joy was pregnant and didn't want the baby. You wanted the baby, and lucky for you, you had some leverage over her to make her have the baby. Now, what cards could the Boy Genius play? This part gets a bit involved, so try to follow along," he smiles big.

John really **needs** to punch him.

"Maybe right after 9/11 the Feds started developing a covert cyber program. Maybe the program is called FICA. Maybe the

Feds really wanted the mad computer skills of a Boy Genius. Maybe Joy's career hung in the balance of what you decided to do. Now, for the interesting part. Within days of your breakup with Joy, you two reconciled and planned a move to Virginia. Coincidently, Quantico is in Virginia. Nine months go by—that's the amount of time it takes to become an FBI agent, and coincidentally the amount of time it took for the two women in your life to have your kids. Joy delivered her baby first, I figure that's because she was already pregnant when you got Kittridge pregnant, but that's a story for another time. So, Joy had her baby, you got custody of the baby. You brought the baby back to Massachusetts and you opened Netti Barn—as your employment cover. You moved Kittridge and the girls into Netti Farmhouse where you knew they would be safe. You and Kittridge raised the kids, while you and Joy secretly led lives as super-spies. How am I doing, so far?"

John breaks his silence, "Good night, Fred." He walks away—then stops dead in his tracks.

"Tell Joy the MFPD welcomes her back to Mayflower."

Who's a Fed?

Fred satisfied the hell out of Kitt in bed the night before—he knows he is going to have to satisfy her curiosity this morning. He jumps right in, "Okay, this is what I think. The Boy Genius and his girlfriend were recruited by the FBI or CIA while at UMass. They became distant and squirrelly, which is expected of them as recruits. They broke up at graduation—I figure Joy was pregnant and didn't want the baby..."

Kitt begins shaking her head. "Joy got pregnant after me."

"Nope. And don't interrupt," he smiles wide.

Kitt folds her arms across her chest, "You can be quite demanding, you know."

"I know. And you didn't seem to mind last night." Fred's cell rings – he takes the call – Kitt takes a quick trip down sexual lane.

"Kittridge," he growled her name as he moved toward their bed.

"Yes, Fred."

"Are you naked?"

She pulled back the sheet, "Naked and eager." Kitt moved close and nestled into him the second he hit the sheets. She left a trail of tiny kisses across his shoulder, pressed her chest against his, moved her belly against his length. In one fell swoop, Fred wrapped Kitt in his arms and rolled her beneath him. A gleeful noise escaped her lips.

What Fred Serpico and Kitt Mahoney have in bed shouldn't be thought of as having sex, or even making love—their "thing" is so much more than what either of those trite expressions conjure up. From their first time together, it was clear that they were made for one another. They just fit.

Kitt closed her eyes, and pulled a shaky breath at his first touch. When his hand cupped her breast and found her nipple, she mewed, and when he kissed, sucked, and nibbled, she whimpered. The wanting woman spread her legs, lifted her hips, ran her hands down his back, urged him in. He took control, gathered her hands and lifted them above her head. "Leave them there," his voice husky with desire.

Kitt opened her eyes and watched his lovemaking. Tiny purrs escaped her in response to his kisses, his touches, his gentle probing. Her breathing halted when he found this spot or that zone. Her anticipation fueled her desire, or perhaps it was the other way around. She struggled to obey his directive of no touching, but her need, warm and wet now, pressed against his length, she teased and toyed with her hips, begged on halted sighs, "Please, Fred, please." Kitt shivered when her man found "that place" to pleasure with kisses, touches, and gentle pushes. When he settled in, her release was immediate.

The man who walks back into the kitchen takes one look at his woman, and offers a "Fred Serpico" comment, "Am I interrupting something, Ms. Mahoney? You're a bit flushed, and I believe you may be panting."

"Please, just…"

"I believe I heard that plea quite a bit last night."

Kitt's flush turns to a blush. "Do you have time to…"

"Maybe tonight," he smiles w.i.d.e.

"Do you have time to finish the story?" she exasperates.

"For you, Ms. Mahoney, anything." He means it – she knows it. He starts back in, "Joy gave Tess to John as soon as she gave birth, the question for me was: why would a woman go through a pregnancy if she didn't want the baby?"

"Maybe she didn't want to have an abortion."

"Nope. John wanted the baby. Now, what cards could John play to make Joy stay pregnant? I figure the Feds really wanted the mad computer skills of a Boy Genius and maybe Joy's career hung in the balance of the choice John made."

Kitt thinks Fred is off track. She starts to interrupt, but—

He shakes his head. "I think John and Joy made a deal; they could both become agents if John got custody of their baby. Once the deal was set, they went to Virginia where the training base for the FBI and CIA is located. John didn't travel back and forth between you and Joy, like he said he would—he couldn't, because he wasn't in college, he was in training. He stayed in Virginia, became a Federal agent, Joy had their baby, John got the baby, he came back to Mayflower, opened Netti Barn as his employment cover, moved the Mahoney-Maxwell clan to Netti, set Pentagon-worthy security at a farm, and at a barn, and none of you were the wiser."

A memory from Netti pushes in…"Kitt, you left the farmhouse unsecure, today," he said as soon as he walked in.

"I know. In my defense, John, the sequence is just too long, and difficult. Why can't you choose something simpler like 1-2-3-4?"

"That's not a security code, Kitt, that's a preschool counting lesson. You need to activate security when you leave."

She rolled her eyes, "How about you just worry about the security at Netti Barn. That's where your computers are. There's nothing at the farmhouse that's worth anything."

"You and the kids are at the farmhouse, Kitt. You need to learn how to use…"

"Got it!" she cut him off.

Within a fraction of a second, the – penny – drops. "Oh. My. God. John's a Fed," Kitt exhales the words, as though they have been sucker punched from her.

A silence pushes against them. The silence is quickly broken.

"Who's a Fed?" Annie asks as she joins them in the kitchen.

Fred doesn't miss a beat, "This perp we arrested yesterday ended up being a Federal agent. He was pretty pissed when we screwed up his sting."

"Oh." Annie shrugs in seeming disinterest, grabs a travel mug from the cabinet, fills it with coffee, grabs her messenger bag, and scrambles out the back door, "Gotta go." She throws herself into her Jeep and speeds down Tarrington, "Shit. Shit. Shit. Fred knows about Dad."

Netti
Joy and John were up all night talking, and not talking. They've just crashed when…

"Dad! Dad!" is shouted in concert with several fist bangs on the back door.

John tugs on his jeans and heads to the kitchen. He slides back a chain-link lock seconds before Annie pushes her way in.

"What the hell?"

"Good morning to you, too, Annie."

"Dad, you've got this place wired with more levels of security than the Pentagon. I know every level, and I couldn't get in this morning. Why? Because of a simple chain-link lock," Annie stares at her father.

He stares back.

"You've **never** locked me out before. There's only one reason you didn't want me just coming in. DOA is here, or some other super-de-duper-spy friend of yours is here—which, under normal circumstances I'd let slide—but today is **not** falling into the normal category. Fred just told Mom that you're a Fed."

The enormity of what Annie just said landed like a punch to John's gut—not the part about Fred telling Kitt that he's is a Fed, although that is problematic—but the part where his daughter nonchalantly referred to him as a spy. That hit something deep.

Annie Mahoney-Maxwell learned about her father's double life in 2015. When Kitt Mahoney inherited the beachfront property in Laurel Falls, she embarked on a major renovation on the bungalow. Construction lasted more than a year, and her patience lasted way less time than that. During the final stages of work, the crew allowed her to move things in piecemeal.

"Annie, your father and I are doing a bungalow shuffle and furniture setup."

"Okay."

"John, I'll meet you there. Don't keep me waiting…"

"Right behind you."

While they were in Laurel Falls setting up the mini master for Annie, she was at the farmhouse breaking into John's home office computer systems, and setting wheels in motion, dangerous wheels. When the Special Agent returned home, he found his daughter elbow deep in his FICA systems, and deeper than that in cyberland.

"Get out!"

"Dad."

"Not now! Get out! I need to check…"

The security failure on John Maxwell's part is how Annie learned that her father is a Federal agent—how she learned that Sam Sawyer is his FICA identity—how she learned about a secret agent named DOA. A computer whiz in her own right, Annie spent her childhood at Netti Barn with cyber interns from the best colleges in the world. By the time she was twelve, she was skilled enough to handle software design for Netti Barn's legitimate clients—but, she was a greenhorn, who infiltrated FICA's systems, and left them vulnerable. In doing so, she exposed the preeminent cyber huntress known as DOA to dangerous factions that lurk in the deepest recesses of cyberland. **That** is how Hector found the thread to pull on Joy Ann Watts.

Special Agent Maxwell is the only person who knows that.

You're DOA?

Annie is tapping her toes waiting for her father's confirmation or denial that DOA, or some other spy is at the farmhouse, and doesn't hear Joy enter the kitchen behind her. She doesn't even discern a change in the room, until Joy speaks.

"You know about me." It wasn't a question, although it should have been given DOA is a spy, and all.

Annie turns and comes face to face with a ghost. "You're DOA?" she croaks. John's daughter spins back toward him and accuses, "Joy Ann Watts is DOA?" The – penny – drops. "Oh. My. God. Joy Ann Watts masqueraded as Fee Peterson, the intern you had working at Netti Barn when we were kids. It wasn't Fee who played with me, and cuddled Callie, and Tess. Oh. My. God! It was Joy Ann Watts at Netti, the mother who gave Tess away. You allowed Joy to play with us behind Mom's back. What is wrong with you, Dad? Oh. My. God. Joy Ann Watts is Fee Peterson, and **they** are DOA, the super-spy. I think I'm having a stroke. I hope I'm having a fucking stroke!"

"You seem surprised, Annie," Joy says flatly.

"Not helping, Joy." John makes a move toward his daughter. She puts her hand up to block him, then stands in the middle of the kitchen as though in a trance. Images click through Annie's mind like a slide show.

Click. Her playing outside Netti Barn with Fee. Click. Callie and Tess bouncing in baby seats while Fee read stories to Annie. Click. Fee holding Tess on her lap, and tucking her into the crib in the barn nursery. Click. Fee letting Annie watch and memorize her lightening quick keystrokes at Netti Barn. Click. Click. Click.

Annie looks hard at the woman standing in front her. "You were at Netti Barn the whole time," her words coming on moans. "Right under my mother's nose. My nose. How could we not know that Fee Peterson was Joy Ann Watts, and that you were here, at Netti?" Annie chokes on unshed tears. She looks accusingly at Joy and pains her next words, "And then, one day you were gone. Vanished. Like a ghost. How – why did you leave—without saying goodbye?" She breaks at the memories.

"Fee! Fee! Are you back?" The first-grader bounded into Netti Barn.
John followed behind his daughter knowing it was time to tell her, "Annie. Let's go up to the loft."
"The loft! I'm not allowed in the loft," her excitement finding her big, round eyes.

"Today, you are allowed in the loft."

Before taking to the many, many stairs, she needed to choose which staircase to climb, "I'll go up one, and come down the other."

"That's a very good idea. Which stairs will we climb?"

"Eeny, meeny, miny, moe – catch a tiger by the toe – if he hollers – let him go – eeny, meeny, miny moe." Before she finished the rhyme, her little feet were in motion, "Come on, Daddy!"

Father and daughter climbed the stairs, hand in hand. When they made it to the landing, the little girl pulled her dad with all her might toward the expansive loft window, "Let's look! Let's look!" John held his little one in his arms, and gave her a tight embrace, a preemptive show of support. John knew that in a matter of minutes he was going to break Annie's little heart. He knew it couldn't be helped. They stood quietly, looking out the window—she with wide-eyed wonderment—he with a heavy heart.

"Our farm is big, Daddy."

"It is."

"How big?"

"Fourteen acres."

"What's an acre, Daddy?"

"It a measurement of land."

"A big measurent?"

"Yes," he laughed.

"Is our farm big enough for cows?"

"Yes."

"And horses?"

"Yes."

"And ponies," she turned hopeful eyes his way.

"You're not getting a pony, Annie."

"Okay." She cuddled in for another minute or two, then asked, "Where's Fee?"

John set her on her feet, and took her little hand in his, "Let's go sit on the fluffy couch, I have something to tell you. Fee had to…"

"…but she didn't say goodbye." After a heartbreaking cry, the little girl got up from the fluffy couch. "Can we go downstairs?"

John nodded and took hold of Annie's hand. He stopped when they got to the landing.

Annie lifted her teary eyes upward, "Why did you stop, Daddy?"

"Just waiting for you to tell me which staircase we'll use on our way down."

Annie didn't bother with choosing, or with nursery rhymes, she simply said, "It doesn't matter, Daddy."

Annie Maxwell-Mahoney never asked to go to the loft, again.

Joy takes a step toward Annie.

Annie takes a step back.

Joy answers her questions.

"The *how* is that I never worked at Netti Barn when your mother was around—I changed my appearance so no one would recognize me—you were a kid. The *why* is that your father and I were building FICA, and when we were finished, I went Dead On Assignment."

"DOA," Annie whispers. She had long since lost any measure of emotional control, and is now physically trembling from the shock of things. John steps toward her, "No," she croaks.

He steps back. "Let's take a break." Joy heads to John's bedroom, Annie heads to the staircase opposite the front door, it's the place she always went when she was upset. She climbs halfway up, sits on the fifth stair from the top, and is rewarded with, "the squeak" and a memory.

"Annie Mahoney-Maxwell," her mother called out from the kitchen.

"Yes."

"Are you eavesdropping from the front stairs, again?"

"Yes."

"We have discussed this matter, have we not?"

"Yes."

"What have you to say for yourself?"

"That you should get this stair fixed, or I should sit on a different one."

Annie smiles at the memory, then breaks into tears, the ones she stopped shedding after that day in the loft.

John heard the squeak from the kitchen, then listened to his daughter's pain being cried away. He steps out onto the back porch. While there, he calls Kitt, "Hi."

"Hi."

Silence.

"Can you keep Callie and Tess at the bungalow for the rest of the week?"

"Yes."

Silence.

An uncomfortable distance settles between the two lifelong friends. Her distance is filled with unasked questions. His distance is filled with untold truths. Neither says anything more before disconnecting.

John Maxwell assess where he is in his life. He wants to explain how he brought all of them to where they are. Sam Sawyer will never explain—he can't. The Special Agent accepts that people are beginning to learn that John Maxwell is a Federal agent—that's bad. If Fred keeps digging, people will learn that John is Sam Sawyer, a covert agent, the preeminent defender of cyberland—that will be deadly. And once Kitt learns that Annie knows about his duplicity, has known for years, all bets are off. There is no telling what her reaction will be because no one has ever betrayed Kitt the way Annie and John have.

Focus on the game.

After his phone call with Kitt, John heads to the barn to review the interns' work. He summarily dismisses them from service, "I've got something to deal with, so enjoy the next couple of weeks off. I'll call you." On his way out of the barn, he sees Annie leaving by way of the front door—without so much as a goodbye. He walks the length of his property, stands on the driveway, and watches until her orange Jeep disappears down Farm Road Low. The increasingly pissed-off man heads back inside the farmhouse, goes to his room, finds Joy in some sort of yoga pose on the floor, scoffs and says, "Follow me." He storms across to Netti Barn, slams the door, and locks them inside. "The loft." She leads. He follows. They sit opposite one another, "Tell me about Hector. More specifically, tell me about the game," he directs.

"I'm tolerating this bullshit attitude, John, because you've had a go of it this morning, but don't push me." She scowls. She stares. She submits. "Like I said before, Hector has been bugging the crap out of me for two years, mostly nuisance stuff. This summer, things changed; he became intense."

"Explain."

"Let me give you an analogy. For two years, Hector courted me. He let me know that I was special to him by spending as much time with me as he could. Then, bam, he got serious. He wanted to claim me as his. I pushed back. He gave me an ultimatum in the form of a game; I needed to find him and kill him, or he was going to find me and kill me. Then, he was going to kill Sam Sawyer."

"Why didn't you contact me?"

"At first, I thought this was about me, or rather, I thought it was about the preeminent huntress of cyberland. Everyone hunts DOA, so I thought the cybermenace was nothing more than a hunter on steroids. I contacted Director Gaffney, and told him about the menace. He was pissed, and acted like I'd fucked up, or done something to entice the menace. When I told him that the menace identified himself as Hector, the cyber-drug-menace, Gaffney did an about-face. He said it was good that Hector was after me, and that he identified himself to me. He said it gave FICA an advantage, one they hadn't had before. In response to that, Gaffney put FICA agents in the depth to find the menace. He sent me on a fake assignment, tipped the agents off to where I'd be, and had them lay in wait for Hector. Gaffney's divers couldn't keep up with me or him, and were essentially ineffective. By then it was summer, and that's when Hector switched it all up and referred to **you** as his nemesis. That's when I realized that this is about the both of us. I'm not sure what the catalyst was for Hector to take such an interest in me, or why or how he connected me to Sam Sawyer, but whatever it was, it happened a couple years ago..."

"Forget about that. Focus on the game."

"We should examine this through the filter of FICA, John. We both work for…"

"Joy. Focus on the game."

"Hector issued an August 1 begin date and an October 13 end date on the game. The start date bothered me because that's when you and I always start our time together. It made me wonder if Hector had access to the alphabetical reunion list. That's why I didn't meet you in Madrid."

"Go on."

"I was already on vacation from FICA, so I went completely off the grid. I traveled to the West Coast, got my things in order, and went low for a few days. Then I traveled to Boston, got a new computer system, holed up in a hotel, and tried to figure this whole mess out. I changed my cyber signature, so I could dive deep without anyone knowing I was there. I reviewed every freaking keystroke I made two years ago, looking for whatever it was that I did that put Hector on my trail. I came up empty. Then I began doing old-school research on Hector, the meaning of the word, and the name. I sort of already knew what the word meant, still I was amazed at how neatly it fits to the actions of the cybermenace. The word, hector, is a verb, and it means to irritate, taunt, bully, torment, and threaten. The cybermenace has done all those things to me, and pretty much in that order. I didn't get much from that so I started researching Hector from Greek and Roman mythology."

John smiles. She stops her dissertation.

"What?"

"Just enjoying how your mind works. Please, continue."

"In Homer's epic poem, *Iliad*, Hector commanded the Trojan army. He became an inexhaustible defender of the ancient city of Troy. In an attempt to defeat his greatest rival, Achilles, Hector needed to go beyond the walls of the city—at which point, he became a hunter. As he set out, he had a premonition that he would die in battle with Achilles. He took solace in knowing that in death he would be celebrated as the greatest defender **and** the greatest hunter known to the people of Troy. I think our Hector is a nut job who thinks of us as his Achilles. If he succeeds in taking us out, he will be celebrated as the greatest defender and hunter known to cyberland."

John nods, "What else?"

"I haven't been in touch with FICA since August 1. They've probably listed me as a defector—unless you've told them that I'm using the last resort."

"I have not." He lies.

Bullet Bungalow

Annie is surprised to find Fred's truck still at the bungalow when she pulls onto the driveway. Almost simultaneously, Fred rounds the corner from the porch and Annie hops out of her Jeep.

"Were classes cancelled?" the man asks.

"What? Oh, classes. Yeup, they were cancelled."

"All of them?" the detective asks.

"Ah…not all of them, but enough, so I decided to blow off the rest." Annie sets about unclasping this and disengaging that as she readies to remove the Jeep's doors, and roll back its soft top.

"Need any help?" the querying man queries.

"Nope. I've got it," she says as she leans the removed door panels against the bungalow, and straps sections of the roof in place.

"Looks like you're hitting the road."

"You're good at this detecting stuff, Serpico."

He smiles and agrees, "I am, Ms. Mahoney-Maxwell. Right now, I'm detecting that you're a bit pissed off about something, and you're about to put some distance between you and whatever happens to be pissing you off."

"Yeup." The look she sends the detective's way suggests that he is the something that's pissing her off. Annie hops into her Jeep, clutches, shifts into reverse, and backs out onto Tarrington. "I'll be back late."

Fred experiences his first ever ping of parental concern, "Well, that's new."

Cutters Cove

Annie presses the buzzer for condo 2A. "Your Harley and your Tacoma are here, so..." She waits a couple minutes, buzzes again, and is just about to leave when she hears his voice.

"This better be good, whoever you are."

"Mike, it's Annie. Do you want to go on a road trip?"

"If you're driving. I pulled a late shift last night."

"I'm driving. I'll be waiting in the Jeep. Five minutes, Monopoli."

"This is some damned way to wake up..." Annie hears him say as she walks away from the buzzer pad.

Same Atlantic, different oceans.

Fred has been pacing his office for hours—an unusual turn of events. His partner is out of the station with Officer Speil on an instructional assignment, and isn't expected back until late afternoon, so Fred is burning off some energy. As soon as Detective Phelps walks in, Detective Serpico starts in. "When I got to the farmhouse last night, John was standing outside, clearly annoyed that…"

Steve listens to the recount as he paces the office, then he starts in. "And John never denied anything?"

"Nope. He didn't say a single word, until he told me to leave."

"And Joy. Do you really think she's in town?"

Fred pauses a second. "Do I think it? Yes. Do I have anything concrete to go on? No. What I've got is circumstantial, at best, but John's reaction when I told him to welcome Joy back to Mayflower—that was big. I'm telling you, Steve, John doesn't have a single 'tell'. Granted, it was dark outside, but there was enough ambient light for me to see him. John Maxwell didn't so much as flinch, blink, or alter his breathing when I presented what I'd pieced together. Honestly, there was **nothing** until I made the comment about Joy—**that** definitely got to him."

Steve takes a single pace around the office and proclaims with certainty, "Joy's in Mayflower."

Fred heads to the window, takes a pondering look around, and agrees, "Joy's in Mayflower." Fred waits a couple of minutes then adds, "There's more."

"There always is, Fred."

"I talked to Roni before I headed to John's. I told her I needed some help. She was eager to help me—until I asked for information on John Maxwell and Joy Ann Watts."

"And ..." Steve prompts.

"Roni took a breath."

"And ..." Steve prompts.

"The breath. It's Roni's 'tell'. She knows John and Joy, I'm sure of it. She flat-out denied knowing them, then she ripped me a new one when I mentioned their names. She told me in no uncertain terms to leave whatever I was doing alone. She hung up on me."

"Damn, Fred. This keeps getting bigger and deeper. Do you have any idea what we're dealing with?"

"We?"

"I'm in, man. Whatever this is. Whatever you need." Steve smacks Fred's shoulder. "By the way, does Kitt know about Veronica?"

"Nope."

"None of it?"

"Nope."

"Better get on that, Fred."

I-95N

"Where are we going?"

"To the beach."

"What beach?"

"Short Sands in York, Maine."

"Annie, you live at the beach. You can literally step out your back door, and be knee deep in the ocean."

"The ocean in Maine is different than the ocean in Massachusetts ... Oh for fuck's sake, did I just say that?"

Mike laughs, "Yeah. Why?"

"Nothing," Annie groans, "it's just some stupid shit I picked up from my mother," she groans again.

"*My* ocean," Kitt sighed as she looked out at the playful waves meeting shore at her place in Laurel Falls, Massachusetts. The native New Englander grew up with sand, surf, and sea as part of her life, so it's safe to say that she knows a thing or two about the Atlantic Ocean. And what she knows is that the ocean in Laurel Falls is different than the one in Mayflower. It's also safe to say that Annie had strong opinions on that subject.

"Mom, of all the hair-brained theories you've come up with, this is the whopper. The Atlantic Ocean in Mayflower is the same Atlantic Ocean in Laurel Falls. In fact, I can prove that point with a float, some waves, and an undertow."

It was usually at that point in their back and forth that the daughter was handed a float, along with a bit of attitude from her mother, "Have at it, Miss Mahoney-Maxwell."

The two Maine beachgoers sit on a bench that overlooks the quarter mile pocket beach that's tucked between rocky cliffs in the tiny village of York. After a few minutes of relaxing, Mike treads in—to the conversation—not the ocean. "So, what's up, Annie?"

She shrugs, "I needed to get away. I wanted to be with you."

Mike chuckles.

"What?" she nudges.

"You're consistent, I'll give you that."

She stares blankly.

"This thing between us is nothing but starts and stops. You want me, but you can't be with me because you need me. Want – need – I don't understand why it matters, but somehow, you've twisted that shit up in your head and made it so we aren't together."

"Yeup." She looks away, and points to a tiny islet, "That's Cape Neddick Lightstation, most commonly known as, Nubble Light. It's been in service since 1879, and it's the most photographed landmark in Maine."

Mike takes Annie's hand. "Let's go take some pictures of the lighthouse, grab some dinner, and go back to my place. Maybe we can concentrate on wanting each other for a while, and see what happens."

Annie smiles.

Mike smiles.

Bullet Bungalow

Kitt is pacing the back porch when Fred arrives home. It is well past sunset, and she hasn't seen or heard from Annie since she flew out of the house for Littleton that morning. Kitt was just about to call John when Fred bounds up the stairs. "Have you seen Annie?" she starts right in.

"Not since this morning. Why?"

"She hasn't been home, hasn't returned any of my texts or calls, and her Jeep wasn't on campus today."

"Yeah, about that..."

"About what, Fred?"

"She came back to the bungalow this morning. She said that a couple of her classes were cancelled, and she was blowing off the rest. She was in a mood, Kittridge. She took the doors off the Jeep, rolled the top back, and said she'd be back later. You didn't see half of her Jeep leaning against the bungalow," he smiles.

"You let her leave? Even though she was in a mood?"

He laughs, "What could I do, Kittridge?"

"Nothing, but is there something you can do now?"

Fred nods, "Let me make a couple calls."

Kitt is kneeling on the porch sofa when Fred returns. "Her Jeep's been seen around town, so..."

"So, she's alright?" Kitt relaxes.

Fred nods.

The momma-grizzly gets up, storms past him with a, "Good. When she gets back, I'm gonna kill her."

His laugh follows after her, "I'm a cop, you know. You really shouldn't threaten people in my presence."

"I suggest you leave then, Detective Serpico."

Fred doesn't relax until he hears Annie's Jeep pull onto the driveway around midnight. He gets off the couch he's been riding for the past few hours, and heads to meet her, "You're safe."

"Yes."

"Good. Next time let your mother know that."

Annie nods.

"Come on, let's put your Jeep back together."

They work in silence—Annie breaks that silence, "Thanks, Fred."

"You're welcome, Pixie."

Maxwell made contact.

John calls Annie first thing Thursday morning and asks her to meet him at Netti Barn. Against his better judgment, and over Joy's objections, the Special Agent asks his civilian daughter to help with the Hector investigation.

"You want *me* to work with you, and that other spy over there? I must have had a stroke, yesterday."

"Do you want in?"

"Yeup." Annie turns to Joy, "What are your thoughts on this?"

"It's his call," she says before walking away.

Annie turns to her father, "Sooooo, she's not thrilled."

The Special Agent doesn't bite, "This is the plan. Joy will let Hector know she's back in cyberland. She will handle her interactions with him in whatever way she sees fit. Annie, you and I will hack FICA agent files. I'm mostly interested in signs of excessive communication with foreign agents or dark assets."

Annie responds with her familiar childhood retort and a salute, "Roger, Dodger."

"Wait here." John leaves the barn.

Annie smirks at Joy, "Something I said?"

"Nope. He's going for a run. There must be something bothering him."

"Huh. Wonder what that could be?"

"Come on, I'll set you up, and set your diving parameters…"

John sets out on his running trails. He knows that there's something that he needs to work through, although he isn't really sure what it is, yet. "Start at the beginning, find the thread, then pull." He grabs hold of the thread that started the whole mess. "Annie compromised the covert agent known as DOA." **pound, pound, breathe** "Hector started trailing the preeminent huntress." **pound, pound, breathe** "Why was Hector the only nefarious diver who benefitted from Annie's hacking?" **pound, pound, breathe** "He's had a ten year criminal run without being caught." **pound, pound, breathe** "So he's good, or …"

John parks his ass on a mammoth rock by a little stream on the backside of his property, and keeps looking for threads—he pulls them when he finds them.

"Hector's been hunted by the DEA, FBI, FICA, and CIA for years. Every agency has a vested interest in getting the cybermenace out of cyberland. As soon as Hector identified himself to Joy as the cyber-drug-savior, and she reported him to Gaffney, things started happening in rapid succession. The Director's immediate action was to put FICA agents deep into cyberland to track DOA. His calculation: if FICA agents follow DOA, and Hector follows DOA, the agents will get Hector." John pulls the threads that come loose from that assessment. "If Gaffney neutralized Hector that would have been a huge win for FICA, and a huge victory for him, personally. That have would have positioned him nicely for the Director position at the FBI, the next time it came up. It's no secret that Gaffney wants that job—no secret that he was pissed when Shelby Webber got it over him. Good money says that Gaffney didn't tell any of his counterparts that he had a lead on Hector. He went it alone, but..."

John gets up and starts back along the trail. "Putting his agents on DOA's trail backfired." **pound, pound, breathe** "It helped Hector connect DOA to FICA." **pound, pound, breathe** "Once the cybermenace had a connection." **pound, pound, breathe** "He pulled that thread and found out that DOA used to be undercover agent Fee Peterson." **pound, pound, breathe** "That's when he challenged her to the game, and sent her off the grid." **pound, pound, breathe, breathe, breathe, breathe** "Joy needs to get back to ghosting in cyberland. She's safe in the depths. She's not safe at Netti." He pulls a final thread and tosses a question, "Did someone at the Agency accidently lead Hector to Joy, or is someone actively working against the preeminent huntress?"

Washington, DC
"Maxwell made contact."

"And?"

"Watts is in Mayflower. She's hiding at his place."

"Secure her."

"I need to get rid of Hector first. DOA won't be able to work effectively for The Realm if the cybermenace continues to fuck with her in the depths."

"What's your plan?"

"Give Hector what he wants—John Maxwell."

"And?"

"Hector takes out Maxwell. We take out Hector. We take DOA."

Cyberland.

     The worldwide intelligence realm is known as cyberland. It is a vast place—think ocean—actually think of cyberland as being as expansive as all of the world's oceans, seas, lakes, ponds, rivers, streams, and puddles combined. Anyone with a computer—approximately 2 Billion people at last count—can visit cyberland. The majority of the people who enter are World Wide Web searchers. They are referred to as waders or swimmers, and they tend to stick close to the shore, taking a dip here, maybe a dive there. Those who go deep into the abyss are called divers—their skill level determines the depths to which they can go. The ones who can descend as deeply as Joy are the most effective cyber experts in the world. They usually work for governmental agencies and/or criminal organizations. The vast majority of depth dwellers have nefarious reasons for their descent into the abyss—though not all divers are criminals.

     Take Joy Ann Watts for example. She works for the U.S. government, and to a lesser extent, for their allies. The majority of her international work is contracted by the U.K., even though they have their own cyber division, known as MI6. Their top notch team is headed by Andria Covington, a brilliant diver in her own right, but she is no DOA—to be fair, there is no one else who has the abilities of DOA. Therefore, the U.K. requests assistance from time to time. Those requests go from Assistant Inspector General Covington to her FICA counterpart, Director Roland Gaffney. His team channels the heavily encrypted messages to DOA, and she handles the rest, by diving through, over, or under, enemy defense systems. Once she's in, she helps herself to whatever intelligence is accessible, gets the hell out, and deposits it in secure cyber files placed throughout cyberland. Some of the gathered intelligence is beneficial to the U.S., some to their allies—and since the U.S. and the U.K. are strategically aligned on many fronts, the intelligence is used by both governments. Given that Joy Ann Watts is a Dead On Assignment agent, she has never met any of her counterparts, though she knows who most of them are. None of them know who she is—at least that's the way things are meant to be.

London
"Watts just entered cyberland from the FICA systems at Netti Barn."
    "Is she ghosting?"
    "No. She changed up her signature to give her some cover, but she's doing tap and grabs

into FICA agent files. She's got someone in her wake. It's as though DOA is training an agent."

"Tell Andria that I want the two of you on this until DOA is out of cyberland, or I tell you to stop following her."

"Yes, sir."

Netti

After a training session with the preeminent cyber huntress, Annie Mahoney-Maxwell is good to go. The diving team of father and daughter Maxwell spend hours analyzing tap and grab information from FICA files. They come up with very little to show for their efforts—no surprise there since they are spying on the best computer analysts, programmers, and hackers in the world. The work is tedious, so when Special Agent Watts asks Special Agent Maxwell for some defensive moves against Hector, he bails on Annie—she considers that an opportunity to go rogue and dive deep.

FICA

The agent calls his superior. "Maxwell and Watts are deep."

"Is Hector on them?"

"Yes. Should I send in the team?"

"No. There's been a change in plans. We are no longer going to protect Hector from the authorities, and we are no longer going to protect Maxwell from Hector. We are going to sit back and let them destroy each other. Then we are going to get DOA."

"What is my assignment?"

"Follow the Special Agents, and report back."

THE MENACE

Hector jolts when he sees DOA in cyberland. In a nanosecond, he dives deep and starts chasing the preeminent huntress. His heart begins racing when he sees Sam Sawyer start throwing defensive blocks for her. The cybermenace has been on DOA's trail for years—she has **never** brought Sam Sawyer in as her defense. "It's working." He laughs. He keystrokes. He brags. "I told you, Troy, the preeminent huntress and the preeminent defender know each other. Just like I predicted, the game fucked with her head. She went off the grid and hooked up with Sam Sawyer. And now—they are here—and I am here—yes, yes—and you're here, too, Troy. Now shut up!" Hector tries to get around, over, or under the defender. He is aching to get into her wake, to move on her, to ride her. "Stop distracting me, Troy." "Hector, you need to look, right there. Look!"

Hector looks, "Huh, what's this? Or who's this? Looks like the preeminent ones brought a third player into the game." Hector chases the newbie, "Interesting moves. There's something about your signature that seems familiar." Hector ditches DOA and Sawyer and follows the neophyte.

Lured by the Devil.

Kitt is having dinner with Callie and Tess when Fred gets home. He pulls a seat to the table and helps himself to a square of lasagna. "Been banging pots again, Ms. Mahoney?"

"I have," she smiles wide at his reference to her favorite cooking saying.

"Where's Annie," he asks before sending a forkful of food into his mouth.

"Having dinner with a *friend*," the teenagers singsong in unison.

Kitt laughs and explains, "These two songbirds think there's a romance going on between Annie and Officer Monopoli."

"I can see that." Fred nods his head toward the girls. "Mike's a good guy. He'd treat Annie right. But Annie's not with Mike. I just saw him at the station; he's on until midnight."

"Awwww," Callie and Tess whine in unison.

Down on Main Street
Lynn McAvoy leaves the Center in the capable hands of her assistant, and heads home. When the bus passes the MFPD, she makes a decision, "It's time to call Detective Steve."

Steve Phelps and Lynn McAvoy go back a long way, long before Steve became a detective. Lynn dated Steve's older brother, Joe, all through high school. She would be Steve's sister-in-law if not for 9/11. Twenty-year-old, Joe Phelps, enlisted in the Army almost before the second tower fell—Steve would have enlisted right along with him if he'd been of age.

"I enlisted."

"What about Mom, and Lynn?"

"They'll be pissed."

"What if something happens to you, Joe?"

"They'll have you."

When news about Joe hit—it hit hard. Joe's parents were devastated—his girl was destroyed. Steve put his pain aside and focused his energy on helping those Joe left behind. He became the perfect son, and Lynn's rock during the wake and funeral. The kid brother grew up overnight from the news of his brother's death—the broken-hearted girlfriend, went gray overnight from the shock of it. Lynn keeps her hair gray because it is a constant reminder of what she's lost, not that anything could ever make Lynn forget Joe.

"Detective Phelps," he answers the call.

"Hey, Detective Steve, it's Lynn."

"It's been a long time, Lynn. How are you?"

"You know," she says with a touch of melancholy in her voice.

"Yeah. I know." Steve pauses. The space between the two is suddenly filled with Joe. Steve is quick to fill that space with something else. "So, Lynn is this a friendly call, or can I help you with something?"

"Both, Detective Steve."

The friends catch up for a few, then the director of the Care Center fills the MFPD detective in on the new woman—how Lynn had seen her for weeks—how she approached her last Friday to offer her a room and some food—how the new woman came to the shelter for three nights—how she disappeared.

"Well, Lynn, once someone's on the street, it's hard to come in. You know that."

"Yeah, Steve, but she doesn't sit on the bench anymore, either."

"What bench?"

"The one across from the high school. The new woman sat on that bench every morning for weeks, and now she's gone."

Detective Steve Phelps gets off of his slack-ass recliner and starts pacing.

Netti

John walks Annie to her Jeep shortly before 10 PM. He watches as she pulls onto Farm Road, and listens as she speeds away. He hangs outside for a few minutes, getting lost in his thoughts.

"Annie, go to your room. Do not discuss this with anyone. Is that clear?"

"Yes." She made it as far as the doorway, "Dad."

He gave her his annoyed attention. "What?"

"Can you believe that I did that? I mean, that I can do that?" She waited for his response. She is still waiting.

Special Agent Maxwell didn't answer his daughter because he was astounded that his kid had the skill-set to do what she did—infiltrate a FICA system. The day Annie Mahoney-Maxwell outed the Special Agent known as DOA, was the day that John realized Annie is a Girl Genius. It was also the day that he forced his daughter into the role of secret-keeper. Until yesterday, the father-daughter duo had not spoken a word about her hacking a Federal computer system, or anything about John's job. Even when Annie showed a budding interest in working for the Agency, John steered her toward a law degree, without going into detail as to why he was opposed to her working for any of the Federal law enforcement agencies. It was clear to John though, that Annie had been lured by the Devil.

Before the guilty party speaks.

Fred is experiencing indigestion. The cause of his intestinal discomfort isn't the two squares of Kitt Mahoney's lasagna he had at dinner, it's the upcoming conversation he'll have with the chef. Fred nestles close and pulls her close, tucks her head onto his shoulder, and brushes her hair back and away. He stares at his woman, his beautiful woman. "Kittridge, I was thinking about our faux date and how we turned it into a faux, faux, date. Remember?"

She sighs, "Mmmmm."

"And how we really got into the whole 'tell me about yourself' part?"

A chuckle from Kitt, "Mmmmm."

"And how I said that one of the reasons my ex-wife and I split was because there were too many years of undercover work?"

"Yes," Kitt answers rather flatly.

"And you assumed that I was the one who did the undercover work, seeing as I'm a detective and all."

"Yes," Kitt answers rather firmly.

"Well—the undercover work was done by Veronica."

"Huh." Kitt gets up from bed and walks to the darkened window. She looks out at the nothingness in front of her.

"You're picking up my habits, Kittridge. Why don't you come back to bed?"

"Why are you telling me this?" she asks, still staring at the nothingness.

"Veronica Shields is a DEA agent. She knows John and Joy."

Kitt turns from the window. She has a look on her face that Fred hasn't ever seen before.

He changes his mind about her coming back to bed. "Maybe you should look out the window for a few more minutes," he laughs.

She does not laugh. She folds her arms across her chest and begins tapping the toes of one foot. "And how did you find out that Veronica knows them, Fred?"

"I asked her."

"When did you ask your ex-wife about John and Joy?"

There is a long pause before the guilty party speaks. "Last night, before I went to talk to John."

"I think you and I are about to have a talk, Fred."

"Yes, dear," he smiles.

She does not smile. "Let's start with why you thought the three of them might know one another."

"John and Joy stopped seeing you and Annie when they went back to UMass after Christmas break. I figured that's when they were recruited by the Feds, and put into training. That's the way it went down for Veronica."

"A post-it." The UMass senior knew instantly that the neon pink slip hanging from her apartment door was from her landlady. She pulled the note free, and ran back downstairs. She knocked on her landlady's door, then proceeded to bounce on the balls of her feet. She smiled wide when Mrs. Flores opened the door.

"Hello, Veronica, wait here." The landlady crossed the room and was back, waving an envelope as she announced, "It's from the Drug Enforcement Agency. I couldn't help but notice the return-address, and the mailman made me sign for it. It's a thick envelope. I bet that means that you've been accepted."

"May I come in?"

"Of course."

The two women stood and stared at the envelope, or maybe they were staring at Veronica's shaking hand. "You should sit," Mrs. Flores said. "Whatever the news, it's going to be a shock."

Veronica sat. Veronica handed the envelope to her landlady. "You open it."

"Are you sure?"

"Yes, please."

The landlady's smile confirmed the news a fraction of a second before her words, "You're in."

There was an almost indiscernible intake of air seconds before, Veronica Shields, the newest DEA recruit, went flying upstairs to the apartment she shared with Fred Serpico. "I'm in!" she squealed.

"...right after that, she started weapons training. Federal recruits need to be licensed to carry concealed before they get to Quantico. When I was trying to figure out why John carries, I checked out when he got licensed. John, Joy, and Roni got their CCWs during the same time period—when they were seniors at UMass. There were enough parallels between the three of them that I just made the assumption they would have met up at some point during their time at Quantico. I figured right," he smiles wide.

Kitt turns back to the window. "Would you mind giving me a few minutes?"

It didn't really sound like a request, so Fred leaves the bedroom and literally bumps into Annie who's doing her best to sneak in. "Hey, Annie we missed you at dinner."

"Dinner...right...I   had   plans...with Mike...you know...Monopoli...we had dinner."

"A late dinner," Fred helps clarify—or set the trap.

"What? Oh, right…a late dinner. Well, gotta go, I'm exhausted," Annie scurries the rest of the way to her mini.

"Exhausted from lying," Fred grins. He gives Kitt a few more minutes, then knocks before heading back into the master. "Annie's home," he says hoping to lift a bit of the tension that hangs in the air like an anvil that's poised to drop.

"Good. Did she say where she's been?"

"She said she had dinner with Mike."

"I thought you said Mike was working until midnight."

"He is. Annie's lying."

"Of course she is. Lying has become epidemic around here," she snips. "Next you're probably going to tell me Annie's a spy," she huffs on her way to the en suite.

Fred chuckles, but not for long. "No. No way. John wouldn't get Annie involved in this. Would he?" The detective goes to the bedroom window for a lengthy look out at the nothingness.

A good finger, by the way.

Fred answers his cell just as he and Kitt are heading out the door for the day. "I'm on my way in, Steve."

"Is Kitt with you?"

"Yeah."

"Ask her if she has a picture of Joy."

"She heard you, and she's holding up a finger, a good finger, by the way."

"Bring it."

"The finger?"

"The picture. I'm at the shack." He hangs up.

Kitt pulls her "John Box" from the closet shelf for the second time that week. She rummages through a stack of pictures until she finds the one with Joy. It's a great shot of her with John. They are smiling big, and look happily in love. Kitt hands it to Fred.

"Wow. She's pretty. She looks like the actress in *Mamma Mia!* the one who's not Meryl Streep."

"Amanda Seyfried is the actress, and Joy is her doppelganger." Kitt looks at the picture again, "She is really pretty. Of course, that picture was taken when she was fun Joy, not hostile Joy. I'd forgotten how pretty she is," Kitt reflects.

Fred studies the photo. "I have no idea what crawled up Steve's butt about Joy, but it must be big. If he's on to something, this picture can be age enhanced and be very helpful. Kittridge, why did you keep this picture? You know, with all the bad feelings between you and Joy."

"It's for Tess. In case she ever wants to know what her mother looks like."

Fred pulls Kitt close, "You are a wonderful woman, Kittridge Mahoney."

She is just about to close the box when Fred points to the stack of postcards tucked into a corner, "What are those?"

"Postcards from John's annual business-vacation trips."

"What trips?"

"The ones he takes every August. He's usually gone the whole month. It's sort of a resting phase before the school year starts and he gets tied down with Callie and Tess."

"Who goes away with him?"

"No one. He travels alone. Although I tease him that he meets up with some mysterious lover."

"He's gone for a month?" Fred flips through the postcards reading the names out loud, "Athens, Berlin, Calgary, Dublin, Edinburgh, Florence, Genoa, Helsinki, Ica, Jakarta, Kyoto, Lisbon."

Kitt drops the box, sending its contents scattering across the floor. "The alphabet! John has been traveling the alphabet? That can't be a coincidence. Can it, Fred?"

He starts to say something, then stops when Kitt raises her hand. "John didn't travel alone. He met up with Joy—she is his mystery lover. I'm going to kill him!"

"If it's all the same to you, Kittridge, I'm gonna pretend I didn't hear that."

Minty's Shack

Fred meets Steve at his place on the outer limits of Mayflower at the tail end of Slater. No one identifies the road as Slater Road anymore—it's just Slater, and it ends at a heavily tree-lined peninsula along the tail end of Cutters Cove, which is referred to as The Cove. The only thing out that way that's actually called by its full name is Minty's Shack. The old sea-weathered wooden structure sits on a grassy section of a peninsula which is surrounded by a rocky ledge that disappears into The Cove. Steve bought the ramshackle structure for a song, and for the past two years he's been renovating it. Minty's Shack is as desolate a piece of property as anywhere in Mayflower, and Steve loves it.

Fred sprints onto the four-sided wrap porch with Seger's *Night Moves* on his lips. He opens the door, and joins Steve on one of two slack-ass recliners inside.

"Do I have something for you!" they say in unison.

"Go, ahead," again, in unison.

"No, really, you go," annoyingly in unison.

Fred growls in frustration and hands Steve the picture of Joy.

"Wow! She's beautiful. She looks like....." he comes up blank.

"The actress, Amanda Seyfried," Fred fills in the blank.

"Yeah. Beautiful woman. Anyway, a friend of mine, Lynn McAvoy, is the director of Mayflower Care Center, the shelter on Main. She said a fake homeless woman had been camped out for weeks on a bench across the street from the high school—the high school Callie and Tess attend—the high school John drives to every morning. Lynn pegged the woman as being someone who was hiding, not someone who was homeless. Still, Lynn gave the woman a place to stay. After three nights, the woman left the shelter. The fact that she hasn't been back doesn't cause Lynn concern, but the fact that she hasn't been seen on the bench again is very concerning to her. Your turn."

Fred fills Steve in on the alphabet sojourns John took every August for the past thirteen years. The reclining detective gets off of his slack-ass and heads to the wrap porch where he begins pacing around the shack. Fred joins him outside and takes a seat at the picnic table. On the third go around Steve begins.

"So, what are we thinking, the business-vacation trips are some sort of lovers' reunions? A once a year bang-your-brains-out rendezvous?" Steve shakes his head and snorts, "I tell you, man, these Feds are a breed unto their own. Let's put the kink fest aside for a minute. You're also telling me that when Kitt found out about the ABC Love Tours, she threatened to kill John. Now see Fred, that's some normal shit, right there."

Fred laughs a little, before adding, "There's something else, Steve."

"There always is, Fred."

He tells his partner about Annie's lie.

"What's the big deal about Annie lying? She's in her twenties. Twenty-somethings lie; usually because they want some privacy. So, she wasn't with Mike Monopoli, and she stayed out a little late without checking in. Annie's a good kid; she's got her head on straight, Fred. Don't go borrowing trouble. Are you thinking that Annie knows John's a Fed and she was with him at Netti Barn?"

"Seems as though **you're** thinking that Detective Phelps."

Steve shakes his head. "Come on Fred. We're talking about John Maxwell. You know, computer genius, super-dad. Even if we're right about him being a Fed, he wouldn't get Annie involved."

"Not on purpose, but what if Annie just fell into the information, somehow? Annie knows her way around a computer, Steve. Remember, it was Annie who broke open the whole 'why is Charles Eaton Alden after Kitt Mahoney' case, by doing computer searches on deeds and stipulations. What if Annie did an innocent search on her father, found something that piqued her interest, and didn't stop until it was too late?"

"And, then what? Annie keeps her mother in the dark, plays mini Fed with her father? I don't know Fred, that looks bad for John. Are we ready to think he's that kind of guy?"

"That's just it, Steve, I don't have any idea what kind of guy John Maxwell is. Neither does Kittridge, and she's known him her whole life."

"Yeah, and she wants to kill him."

Maybe Hector is a team.

Detective Steve enters the homeless shelter, gives Lynn a warm hug, then hands her an eight by eleven sheet of paper. John's face has been cropped from the picture, so the only face that looks back at Lynn is Joy's.

"That's her. She's older, now. Maybe add a decade or so, but she's still as pretty. She's not as freely expressive as in this picture. In real life, she looks haunted, or maybe hunted is a better word."

Steve mutters on his way out, "Now that we know for sure that she's in Mayflower, she's gonna be hunted."

Netti

John can barely drag himself from bed Friday morning. He shuffles into the kitchen, puts his cell on the counter, and runs a hand through his hair. "What the hell day is it?" he mumbles.

Joy gets up from the kitchen table and makes him a mug of coffee, "It's Friday."

"Annie's not working with us, today."

"No?"

"She ran into Fred when she got home last night. She felt a vibe."

"Hmm."

"Explain your non-comment comment, Joy."

"I have some questions, first," she says rather curtly.

He sips his coffee and waits.

"When did Annie learn that you're a Fed? Does she know how deep undercover you are? What does she know about me? Is she working with Hector?"

John spits most of his coffee across the room and chokes on the rest. More than a minute passes before he bothers answering her questions, and when he does there is annoyance in his tone. "Annie learned that I'm a Fed when she was in high school. She knows about my double identity, but nothing more. Until the other day she only knew that DOA was an agent I work with. As for Annie working with Hector, are you insane?"

"I'm observant."

"Explain."

"Hector was screwing with me, yesterday. I wanted him to see that you and I banded together, so I called you into the hunt. Annie was supposed to be working on FICA agent files, but she went deep and off in another direction from where we were. Hector left me and started following her. Hector has **never** left me. He floats until I enter cyberland, then hops into my wake, and stays there until I outrun him or surface. When Annie showed up, he took off after her. Why? What was it about her being in cyberland that Hector found interesting enough—to leave me? Annie could be working with Hector. It would explain why we can't find him. Maybe Hector isn't only one person, maybe Hector is a team."

"For fuck's sake, Joy. Annie has a personal laptop and a college computer lab at her disposal. She's not on some cybermenace team."

"She has access to your systems, in the farmhouse and Netti Barn."

"Annie is **not** on Hector's team. Besides, we have nothing to indicate Hector even has a team."

"Okay, but answer this question. When Annie went deep, where did she go?"

"I don't know," he says as he pounds a sequence of numbers on his security pad and storms out of the farmhouse.

Littleton College
Annie moves aimlessly from class to class, sits mindlessly in each one of them, grabs a seat at the base of a mammoth oak on the quad, and waits for the campus crowd to thin a bit. She heads to the cafeteria, grabs a quick bite to eat, then heads to the computer lab. She finds it empty, just as she thought it'd be. "It's Friday night, of course it's empty." She makes her way to her favorite terminal, and boots it up. "The systems are nothing like the ones at Netti Barn, but they'll do." The computer analyst on a mission reads her notes,

then runs search, after search, after search. She makes a few notations at the top of each printed run, "School, last name, year of graduation." When she's compiled what she needs, she goes deep. Not as deep as she went yesterday at Netti, but deep enough that few can find her. The Littleton College student is so lost in thought, that she doesn't hear anyone join her in the lab. She jumps a mile when she realizes she is not alone.

"Sorry I startled you, Annie. I just came to lock up the lab."

The young woman puts a hand to her beating heart, and sighs heartily, **"Cluster. Thank God it's you."**

"Are you alright? You seem spooked."

"No, no, I'm fine. I was just really into my computer work." She quickly gathers the pages and pages of printouts and begins stuffing them into her messenger bag.

"Well, if you're done here," Cluster begins, "I can lock up and walk you to your car. You really shouldn't stay here this late, Annie, but if you have to, come get me to walk you out."

The student and the security guard—the recent assault victim and the recent shooting victim—cross the quad in silent reflection of the events that have bonded them.

THE MENACE

Hector spent hours in the newbie's wake before telling Troy she was there. "The newbie came back. She's got the skills for deep cyber diving, but she's a greenhorn." "What makes you think the diver is female?" "The way she moves. I can always tell when I'm riding the ass of a woman." "You can't tell shit, Hector."

Hector pushed away from his terminal. "She's the one, Troy." "The one what?" "She's the one who gave me the thread to pull on the preeminent huntress. She's the one who steered me to DOA two years ago." "Who is she?" "I don't know, but she's searching for me. Well, two can play at that game. First, let's see where the newbie is diving from." "Littleton College. No shit," they say.

Are you armed?

Annie calls her father's cell, "Dad. We need to talk."

"Where are you?"

"Outside Netti Barn." Annie's hand is shaking when she holds out a single piece of paper. "It's a communication from Hector addressed to the computer lab at Littleton College."

The Special Agent's heart bangs against his chest as he reads it. **BACK OFF! Tell DOA that you are banned from playing the game.** The really pissed off father opens the barn door, "Get in!" He slams the door closed behind them.

Joy jumps from her seat, "What's going on?"

John hands Joy the paper.

She reads Hector's warning and sees that it was sent to Littleton College, "Oh. My. God! Annie, what did you do?"

Anger, humiliation, and choked emotions swirl together as Annie tries to get her story out, "Hector sent me that warning last night. I didn't find it until an hour ago when I was going through the stuff I worked on at the college. When Dad and I were analyzing the agent files, I had a thought: What if Hector is a FICA wannabe-agent? Maybe this wannabe knows about FICA because he was approached in college by Director Gaffney like you two were. Maybe the wannabe didn't make the final cut because the Boy Genius here, took wannabe's slot. Last night, I went to Littleton's computer lab. I ran searches on CICS brainiacs from back in your day. I selected the top five from each college, researched them, and printed out a ton of shit about them. I was going to compare those candidates' qualifications to the Boy Genius to see if anyone came close to getting the job at FICA."

John explodes. "When you went to cyberland from a Littleton College computer, you gave Hector everything he needs to find me. You might as well have drawn him a map to Netti! Dammit all, Annie. No one has ever been able to make the connection between Sam Sawyer and John Maxwell for two very good reasons. The first is because FICA built Sam Sawyer's life from the ground up. His historical background consists of a family tree, which was expanded upon with a carefully constructed life story with birth, educational, and medical records. It contains a listing of extra-curricular activities and achievements, it even has a Little League through high school athletic record, complete with pictures and newspaper stories. For all intents and purposes, Sam Sawyer is a real person, and **he** is the agent who works at FICA. The second reason, the more significant reason why no one has been able to connect Sam Sawyer to me is because **I am the best defensive cyber professional in the world**." John stands to his full height and towers over his daughter. "You just gave Hector everything he needs to find me and to carry out his death sentence—on me, and everyone in this room. For fuck's sake, Annie, this is history repeating itself. You gave up DOA two years ago when you…" He stops his rage, and looks at Joy. He finds what he should find—shock, betrayal, and pain.

"I was trying to help," Annie's words are swallowed in a sob.

"But you ended up helping Hector. As long as he couldn't find me, he couldn't kill me. I made sure he couldn't find me for more than a damn decade!"

"I didn't know that." Annie breaks.

"Neither did I." Joy glares at John.

He storms out of Netti Barn, and takes to the running trails. He enters through the tree line at the northwest corner of the property and starts his punishment. A quarter mile in, he exits the trees and follows the trail that leads over a footbridge and continues along a river to a small hill. He takes the hill—again, and again, and again—then he retraces his steps.

Joy joins him at the halfway point, "John, we have to go back and talk to Annie." She is met with the sounds of pounding feet and sharp intakes of breath. "Annie's on to something," Joy tries again. **pound, pound, breathe – pound, pound, breathe** "We're running out of time, John," Joy pleads. **pound, pound, breathe – pound, pound, breathe** "Hector will kill you, then he'll kill me. Annie's pissed him off. She's going to be his new target." **pound, pound, breathe – pound, pound, breathe**

John picks up his pace, and moves away from Joy. When she returns to the farmhouse, she finds that he is behind closed home office doors, apparently having his ass handed to him by Director Gaffney. When he emerges, she follows him to the kitchen, where Annie is anxiously waiting. He talks. They listen. "I'm going to Bullet Bungalow to tell Kitt and Fred everything. Give me a half-hour head start, then the two of you meet me there."

Annie takes in a sharp breath of air.

Joy pushes out a sharp rush of air.

John texts Kitt and Fred, who are on their way to Evviva Cucina for dinner.
John: Meet me at Bullet Bungalow.
Kitt: When?
John: NOW.

The Special Agent, who is moments away from unmasking himself to the woman he's known and loved forever, waits on the porch at Bullet Bungalow. Normally, he would let himself inside, but he has lost that privilege. He stands and stares out at the Atlantic Ocean, its waves rage-crashing toward the shoreline. "That's appropriate." He takes in the sights, sounds, and smells of the ocean as though it's the last time that...

Kitt walks past John without so much as a glance his way. She waits for Fred to disarm the security system that has befuddled her for weeks. Once they are all inside, Fred asks, "Are you armed?"

"Yes."

"Give me your guns."

"I don't think so, Fred."

"We both need to secure our weapons. My safe is in Kitt's room."

"Why?" he asks pointedly.

Kitt answers his question, "Because Fred is afraid that I might kill you if I manage to get my hands on a gun."

John removes a weapon from the waistband of his jeans and another from the ankle holster that started this whole fucking mess. He hands them to Fred, who removes his own gun from an ankle holster. When the detective returns, the man who's in a shitload of trouble begins.

"My name is John Maxwell. I own and operate a software design company called Netti Barn. My name is also Sam Sawyer. I am an undercover Federal agent working for an FBI cyber agency called FICA. Due to recent events,

I have been unmasked. I have been given the authority from the Director of FICA to answer your questions, provided I secure your secrecy on this matter. Lives depend upon it."

"Your life?" Kitt taunts.

"And Annie's," he answers.

Kitt walks slowly but purposefully to John and slaps him. When he turns his face back, she slaps him, again. And again. And again.

Fred stops her and pulls her into his arms. "Kittridge, he needs to say his piece, so we can protect Annie." Fred turns toward John, "That's why you're here."

"Yes."

The sound of a car door slamming falls heavily in the room. "That'll be Annie."

The daughter of two warring parents steps into the kitchen. She walks to her father's side, and looks her mother straight in the eyes, "I screwed up. I accidentally unmasked a Federal agent. I know you want to kill him, but he is literally being hunted by Hector, and now, so am I."

From the porch comes another woman's voice, "Hector is hunting me, too."

Kitt spins and utters a single word, "Joy."

No sooner had Joy walked into the kitchen when Steve arrives. "Sorry, I'm late."

"I thought you were with Maura and the faux twins," Fred says.

"I asked Steve to come," John explains.

"Well, aren't you full of surprises?" Kitt seethes at him.

Steve addresses Kitt, "Maura and the girls are having a 'girls only' sleepover back at her place. John asked if I could help with a situation. Looks like I'm a little late. Did I miss anything?"

Fred answers, "Just the removing of the guns ceremony, the repeated slapping of the face event, and the computer geek is really a Federal agent announcement. Not anything that big, really. That reminds me, anyone packing needs to give me their weapons. All of them."

Joy looks at John. He nods his head.

"Apparently, there's more than one death threat against me."

Everyone looks at Kitt.

Steve removes a gun from a shoulder holster, Joy removes a gun from the waistband of her jeans and a knife from an ankle strap. Fred makes a second trip to the safe, and returns. "What now, John?"

"Let's move to the living room." They file in as though they are marching toward their executions. When they have taken seats, John begins. "Everyone sitting here has a part of the story that brings us to what's happening, today. The story needs to be told from the beginning. We won't be able to stop Hector unless everyone here knows everything." He pauses and locks eyes with Kitt. "We need to begin with you."

Sheryll O'Brien

She is seething.
Annie turns pleading eyes from across the room, "Please, Mom."

Kitt, Fred, Steve.

Kitt

"Clearly, I don't *know* anything."

"You know more than you think. Tell everyone your story as though none of us knows any of it. When you get to a lie I told you, I'll tell you the truth."

"I won't count on it." She turns angry acorns his way then begins. "John brought Joy to Mayflower during Christmas break his senior year at UMass. We all got along great, and I liked them as a couple. Everything went sideways during spring semester. John stopped coming home and the one time he did he brought a totally different Joy with him. She was uncommunicative and hostile. John was no better, he was guarded and secretive."

"That's because we were recruited by the FBI."

"Yes, John. **Fred** told me," she jabs. "Right before graduation John told me he was going to get his master's at UVA. He had never mentioned that as a possibility, so I was totally caught off guard by his decision. On graduation night, he came to Mayflower without Joy. He was pissed. We got drunk. I got pregnant with Callie. A week later John found out Joy was pregnant."

John starts shaking his head.

Kitt looks him square. "When you came home graduation night, you **knew** Joy was pregnant. Fred said you knew and that's why the two of you broke up, but I didn't want to..."

"I knew."

Annie gasps.

Kitt shakes her head and drills her wetting eyes at John. After a minute, she continues. "John followed Joy to Virginia and stayed with her during her pregnancy. When he came back to Massachusetts, nine months later, he had Tess with him." Kitt is rushing through the last parts of her story, vacillating between anger and sorrow. "Annie, Callie and I moved into Netti Farmhouse with John and Tess. When the kids started school, he did the lion's share of weekday stuff. The girls and I did our weekend things, and hung out during the summers. The summers were important to John, too. That's when he and Joy would alphabetically fuck around the world."

Annie gasps.

John flinches when he hears Kitt talk about his reunions with Joy.

"Yes John, I know about your August trips to Athens, Berlin, Calgary, Dublin, Edinburgh, Florence, Genoa, Helsinki, Ica, Jakarta, Kyoto, and Lisbon. You still owe me a postcard from Madrid by the way. Anything else I know, or think I know, came from Fred." Kitt drills steely cold eyes at the man who's been a part of her life for more than half of it, "I'm done."

Everyone gets Kitt's message.

Fred

"I'm not part of this story, John. I had questions, so I found answers. I'll lay them out, but before tonight is over, I expect you to answer two questions. What prompted you to finally come clean, and how can we help clean up this mess? Wait, I guess I have three questions. Can we clean up this mess?"

"It all comes out tonight, Fred. And I hope we can clean this up, otherwise some of us won't come out of this alive."

Fred begins, "My questions started the night I found out John Maxwell carries a concealed weapon. When I asked him about it, I thought for sure he'd say he was packing so he could protect Kitt and Annie from Charles Alden. Instead, he said he carries in case Joy, a woman he supposedly hadn't seen in fourteen years, ever comes back."

John shakes his head at how quickly things have unraveled since that night.

Fred pulls him back to the conversation, "You still with me, John?"

He nods.

Fred nods. "I started wondering what it was about Joy that made John pack heat. Is she a threat to him? Is she a threat to Kittridge and the girls? Is that why John and Joy broke up? OR does John carry a firearm because he's a cop or something? Let's move on from those questions because there are plenty of others. For instance, why did John and Joy breakup at graduation, get back together, and relocate to Virginia, all within a matter of days? That question led to the really important question— what did they do in Virginia? They **did not** go to UVA for graduate school—but they **did** grow a baby in Virginia—that baby is the linchpin to this whole story."

The detective checks with John, who nods. The detective continues.

"The next round of questions that needed answering were—did John and Joy breakup at graduation because Joy was already pregnant—did Joy not want the baby because it could derail her career—did John have an ace in the hole that forced Joy to have the baby— whatever could John hold over Joy's head? That question was easy to answer—John had Quantico."

He looks to John for the verification he does not need. John gives it to him, anyway, "Yes."

Fred smiles. He deserves to smile. He begins again. "Let's recap, John stopped seeing Annie and Kitt because he was recruited by the FBI for a super-secret cyber program. His girlfriend was recruited into the same program, but she found herself in an unwanted pregnancy situation. A deal was struck—Joy got to be a Federal agent—if FICA got John—and John got the baby." Fred reads the faces of the two people who lived the moments. They nod. "Now, for some miscellaneous questions. How did John afford the Netti property and open a software design company right out of college? Why does the security and surveillance at Netti Farmhouse and Netti Barn rival the Pentagon's? Why did my ex-wife, a seasoned DEA agent become squirrelly when I asked about John Maxwell and Joy Ann Watts? Why did she tell me in no uncertain terms to drop my investigation **after** she denied ever hearing of you two? Why was Annie sneaking in and lying about her whereabouts **after** she heard her mother and me discussing a Fed named John? Did Annie already know her father is a spy, and if so, when, and how did she find out?

"Lastly," Fred stops and waits until he has John's full attention, "in the scheme of things, John, my last question has no bearing on the mess you're in. But man to man I have to ask; did you and Joy have a nice time on your alphabetical reunions while Kitt was being deceived, and holding down the fort?" Fred goes and sits next to Kitt. They clasp hands and thread their fingers together. He winks—she tries to smile.

Steve

"Well, that's gonna be a tough act to follow."

He gets a chuckle all around.

"My role in all this has mostly been as a sounding board for Fred until I got a call from Lynn McAvoy, the executive director of the Mayflower Care Center. She told me about a woman who'd spent three nights at the shelter, then disappeared. She also said the woman stopped sitting on the bench across the street from the high school. My detective skills weren't needed on this one. Fred had been operating under the assumption that Joy was in Mayflower. Lynn's story convinced me Fred was right, but I needed something to show Lynn for a positive identification. I took a long shot and called Kitt, who happened to have a picture of Joy Ann Watts. Lynn identified the woman in the picture as the woman from the shelter and from the bench."

Joy, Annie, John.

Joy

"My birth name is Joy Ann Watts. I am a Federal agent so deep undercover that I am known as DOA, an acronym for Dead On Assignment. When I first joined the FBI, my name was changed from Joy Ann Watts to Fee Peterson."

In a fraction of a second, Kitt charges from the couch. Fred struggles to hold on to her. Everyone else moves between the women. Joy never flinches.

"Fee Peterson!" Kitt screams, "The intern who worked with John at Netti Barn when the girls and I first moved to the farmhouse? The intern who **never** seemed to be at Netti when I was around? The intern who my kids thought hung the moon? The intern who played with them, read stories to them, and bandaged their boo-boos when I was at work?" Kitt turns to the man who betrayed her like no other. "How could you? You knew I didn't want Joy or Fee or DOA or whoever the hell she is, anywhere near Annie, Callie, or Tess. Oh. My. God. Tess. You let Joy be with Tess, to hold and cuddle Tess? Was that fun for you, John? And **you**," Kitt turns back to Joy, "you didn't want that sweet baby. You gave her up for a job. A job that lists you as DOA. If I could get my hands on a gun right now, you would be a different kind of D.O.A., and so would you, John." Kitt storms out onto the back porch.

"Let's put story time from Hell on hold for a few minutes," Fred says as he sprints from the room. He finds his whirling dervish trenching an angry line at the ocean's edge. When his feet find sand, he plops onto it and just watches—and listens.

"Fee Peterson! Fee Peterson! I always wondered about her—not that she could be Joy Ann Watts, but that she was *someone* in John's life—like maybe there was some sort of relationship between the two. Shortly after we all moved into the farmhouse, and my maternity leave for Callie ended, I had to return to work, I would drop off Tess at John's mother's and Callie at my mother's, and take Annie to her kindergarten class. I didn't even know about an intern named, Fee Peterson, until summer break. I was mostly working from home that summer, and when I had to go in to Littleton, I would either do the grandma shuffle, or the kids would stay with John. He dedicated a nursery area at the barn, and did his thing. I was so impressed with how seamlessly he did his dad thing and ran a business. He would always say that his 'work, work' was done by the interns," she scoffs, "looks like we know what kind of 'work, work' his favorite intern did."

"Kittridge."

"What?"

"You've got quite the trench going."

She looks down, "Yeah."

"You feel like sitting?"

"No."

"How about questions. Do you feel like answering some questions?"

"No."

"Carry on, then."

She stops and looks at him, "Here's one for the books. When I went back to Littleton that fall, I was promoted. I did a lot of fundraising stuff, but I took over the special events department, so my schedule wasn't Monday-Friday, nine to five. There were lots of nights and weekends when I would be on campus. That's the time when Annie started talking about Fee, her favorite 'Daddy helper'. I never pressed John about Fee because when I asked about her, he brushed her off as just an intern who helped out." Kitt stops to reflect, and gives her head a good shake, "I was really busy getting acclimated to my new job, and John was picking up a ton of slack with the kids. In my gut I knew I should have asked more questions, but I never pressed the issue about Fee. **What a damn fool!**"

"Hey! You're talking about my woman, show some respect," Fred says as he gets off his duff and moves to Kitt. He steps in front of her, so she has to stop her trenching, "Kittridge.

You trusted John. There's no reason why you shouldn't have."

She nods. Sort of.

"I know you aren't up for questions, but…"

"Go ahead and ask it."

"You thought there might have been something between John and Fee?"

"Yes."

"But you didn't ask him?"

"Not until after she left. John got really sad, almost morose, when she stopped working for him. He didn't snap out of it until…"

"He came back from his first August trip," Fred finishes for her.

"Yes. We called his trip, *Athens in August.* I guess we should have called it, *Athens in Joy.*"

After erupting at Fred, marching the shoreline, and raging at her ocean, Kitt has centered herself enough to return.

Joy waits until Kitt is settled on the couch before moving toward her. The women lock eyes. "Kitt, I should start by thanking you. I am deeply indebted to you for being a mother to Tess—for being her mother. I deceived you, we deceived you when I worked at Netti Barn. I indulged myself with a few stolen moments with my daughter, I can't apologize for that."

Kitt nods.

Joy steps away and begins again, "Everything Fred said is true. Every word. He's a damned good detective to get so much of our life story correct. John was the draw for a new cyber program called FICA. After 9/11, there was a push for interagency investigation and intelligence sharing. On college campuses across the globe, there was a heightened focus on cyber defense. CICS programs started spitting out computer defense specialists at a rate of 75% of the total graduates. Companies were on campus recruiting candidates as soon as winter break ended. The FBI, CIA and DEA were there too, but they did their recruitment on the downlow. Director Gaffney showed up out of the blue and let John know that they wanted him on defense at a new FBI division called, FICA. They wanted me, too, but for different reasons. My focus was offensive cyberattacks. My work is aggressive, fearless, and uncompromising."

"Just like you," Kitt accuses.

Joy ignores the dig. "Soon after John and I finished developing the FICA framework for the offense and defense systems, I went deep into cyberland. I was on my own, working on things that only a handful of people knew about. I was, essentially, a ghost. John didn't know where I was, or what I was doing, most of the time. I'm sure he could have found DOA, but he wouldn't ever risk my cover." Joy pauses and her inflection changes. She shares her focus between John and Annie, "Somehow, a cybermenace named Hector found me..."

Fred interrupts Joy's rundown, "Hector? The cyber-drug-savior? That Hector?"

The Special Agents nod. Joy continues, "Let me explain Hector in more detail for the others, Detective Serpico. Hector is a cybermenace who's been hacking FBI and DEA systems for years. He gathers intel on planned raids—gives a big, old heads up to the drug cartels—they move their product, weapons, and people—the Feds execute a raid, and end up empty-handed. In some of the botched raids, lives have been lost. Beyond all that, Hector did something that no one has done before, he found DOA. The deepest divers in cyberland know that there is a preeminent huntress amongst them. None of them knows who that huntress is—nearly no one knows that the ghost goes by the acronym DOA. Hector found out about me, and after two years of focused work, he found out that DOA used to be a FICA agent named Fee Peterson. Days before I planned on meeting John in Madrid, Hector told me that he and I were going to play a game. There was only one way to win the game—I needed to identify him by October 13 and kill him—or he would find me and kill me. The only way I could avoid playing the game and save myself outright, was to give him the identity of Sam Sawyer. Hector said Sam Sawyer is his Achilles."

Fred interrupts, "Is October 13 significant in the world of computer nerds?"

Armed with only their cell phones, John, Annie, and Joy start researching. Their answers come in rapid succession, "No." "Nope." "Nothing here." The cyber defender states the obvious. "We're only using our cells, we need a computer." Joy makes a move to get hers from the porch.

"Wait," Fred says, "Did Hector ever refer to you as Joy Ann Watts?"

"No."

"But you thought he knew your real name?"

"I wasn't sure at the time he challenged me, so I stayed away from Madrid, but I don't think so now. I've moved around a lot since the challenge, and I haven't picked up any sense that I'm being followed."

"So his scam was to smoke you out," the MFPD detectives say in unison.

Fred turns to John. "Well, it looks like I have the answer to my first question. Hector is what prompted you to come clean?"

John nods. "Annie, you're next."

Annie

"I screwed up. I want you all to understand that before I say another word. Mom, you're going to want to blame Dad for certain things, and that's fair. But the reason we are here right now is because **I screwed up**," Annie holds Kitt's stare until she nods. "I learned Dad was a

Federal agent a couple of years ago. It was when we were doing the bungalow shuffle. One day while Dad was out doing a furniture delivery and set-up, I was breaking into his home office computer systems. I found out that Dad works for the FBI, and that his alias is Sam Sawyer. I also found a connection to an agent named DOA. When I breached his systems, I accidently sent Hector on her trail.

"When Dad found out I hacked into his systems, he went ballistic. Not only was he pissed that I'd disobeyed him by going into his inner sanctum, but also because I created an unacceptable risk to him and to other FICA agents. After an intense conversation, he and I made a pact that I would never reveal what I had learned. He also made it clear that he **would not** discuss his work as an agent or his association with the FBI. When I started looking at majors for college, he pushed me away from computer science and toward pre-law. A couple of times, I suggested I might be interested in law enforcement or the FBI, and Dad firmly suggested I think about something else, anything else, for my life. I honestly put what I knew about Dad out of my mind until I heard you and Fred talking about someone named John being a Fed. I rushed to the farmhouse to warn Dad, and was blocked from getting inside by a stupid chain-link lock. When he finally answered the door, I accused him of having a super-spy inside. That's when I learned that DOA, and Joy Ann Watts, and Fee Peterson are **ALL** the same person. I was pissed that Dad and Joy had pulled a fast one on you and me, but then I remembered they're FBI. The Feds lie about everything, you know?" Annie scans the room.

Everyone but Kitt is nodding—she is shedding silent tears.

"Anyway, after I found DOA at the farmhouse, the three of us went to Netti Barn to begin searching for Hector. Dad and I were hacking FICA agent files when..."

Kitt's sorrow turns to fury in the time it takes to shed a tear, "What do you mean, you were hacking FICA agent files? Annie, before you answer" Kitt turns to John, "if you're such a valuable super-spy, how on earth did a high school kid hack your FBI system?"

A proud father admits, "Annie is a Girl Genius."

John's prodigy remains silent for a minute, then confirms. "It's true."

John walks to where Kitt is sitting, "Do you need a break?" It is the first thing he has said directly to her since he arrived. There is so much that John needs to say, but he knows this isn't the time—he fears there may never be a time. He kneels in front of the woman he's loved his entire life—the woman he has betrayed his entire life. He searches her beautiful acorn-brown eyes and finds nothing but sorrow.

Kittridge Anne Mahoney looks away and whispers, "Annie should finish."

Their daughter rescues them from the moment. "So, this is how I screwed up, again. When the three of us were working the agent files, I had a thought: what if Hector is a FICA wannabe-agent? Maybe this wannabe knows about the secret cyber program because he was approached in college by the Director like Dad and Joy were. Maybe the wannabe wanted into FICA, but didn't make the final cut because the Boy Genius here took wannabe's spot. Maybe the wannabe is pissed and is seeking revenge. So, instead of hacking FICA agent files like I was supposed to do, I went deep for a while. Someone followed my trails. Neither of us did anything threatening, but..." She looks to her father for help.

"You need to tell them."

Annie nods. "I went to Littleton's computer lab Friday night. I ran searches on CICS brainiacs from when the Director of FICA first started looking for recruits. I did a ton of research, and in my rush to leave the lab, I missed a message from Hector. The message was actually a warning for me to back off and to tell DOA that I am not allowed to play the game anymore." Annie hangs her head low and begins shaking. "I led Hector directly to Dad and Joy."

The father pulls his daughter into his arms.

"Dad, if anything happens, I love you and I didn't mean to…"

"Annie, go sit. Let me wrap this up so we can make a plan."

John

"Some of what I say will surprise people other than Kitt. Hector has been after me for more than a decade, he knows me only as Sam Sawyer. The menace began issuing me death threats since my first days at FICA, although I was kept from knowing about them for a period of time." John focuses his attention on the really pissed off agent glaring at him. "Joy, my not telling you about those threats was my first lie of omission—the first of many." He gives her the opening to say something. She remains quiet. She seethes, but she seethes quietly. He continues. "Even though I consider Hector to be a constant threat to me, I am not under attack every minute of every day. In fact, there have been wide swaths of time when he goes off the grid. Two years ago, when I left my systems vulnerable to Annie, she exposed a Dead On Assignment cyber agent. That event gave Hector a thread to pull. That thread led him to DOA then to her undercover name, Fee Peterson. He has been working overtime to find out who Fee really is. Once he has Joy's name, he will learn that she graduated from UMass with a Boy Genius named John Maxwell. That is when he will know who his nemesis is. The truth behind this whole mess is that Hector is a formidable foe of **mine**. His actions have always been about unmasking **me**. It is about so much more than that, now.

"When Hector started pushing deep on DOA to get to me, I suggested that FICA put together a select group of agents dedicated to finding the cybermenace. I am part of that taskforce. There is one defensive agent assigned to my protection. We remain anonymous to one another. The other cyber agents in the group work offensively. They hunt Hector." John stops and does a visual check with Joy. She is pissed! "Joy, you weren't asked to be part of the group because Hector found you. FICA thought you compromised yourself, and I didn't tell them it was Annie who did it—I **had** to protect her. The cold hard fact is this, FICA circled their wagons around me because I am more valuable to them. And I let them do it because Annie is…"

All eyes are suddenly on Joy. Her eyes are fixed tight on her betrayer. The man and woman hold one another's stare while everyone else holds their breaths.

"Joy, you should **slap** him. If you want, I'll **slap** him for you," Kitt offers.

John can tell that Fred wants to laugh. The detective resists the urge. Sort of. The enormity of the personal and professional betrayal leaves

Joy gutted and seemingly suspended in some sort of emotional void, incapable of doing anything more than pulling air. John keeps laying it bare. "When Joy didn't meet me in Madrid, I contacted Gaffney. We suspected that Hector made contact with her, and when she stayed off the grid, FICA suspected that she was dead. I didn't know where she was, but I **knew** she wasn't dead—I would **know** if Joy was dead. As difficult as it was, I waited for her to surface. Before Joy went Dead On Assignment, she and I set a rescue plan. If she were ever outed, or there was a contract put on her, she had a last resort at Netti, a place where she could come for help. When she went off the grid, and into hiding, I started watching for her. I knew she'd eventually come to Mayflower—she did, just as the Alden shit was hitting the fan. It wasn't until the night of Cluster's Thank You party that she made contact. By then, the cover agent known as DOA had been off the grid for more than a month." Again, he addresses Joy. "I contacted Director Gaffney when you came in, even though I told you I hadn't."

Fred interrupts, "I need to run all of this in English. Hector learned about DOA in 2015. He connected DOA to Fee Peterson, a FICA undercover agent. He told her that he unmasked DOA's true identity, but he never used the name Joy Ann Watts. Then he said that DOA has until October 13 to unmask him and kill him, or he will kill her, and then he will kill Sam Sawyer. Do I have this right, so far?"

The agents silent check with one another. "Yes," they answer.

"So Hector lied to DOA. He didn't unmask her, and he didn't…"

Annie interrupts Fred. "I led Hector to my father's doorstep."

John shakes his head, "Timing led Hector to me. It was always just a matter of time."

Annie nods, but her eyes fill.

"The day Annie hacked my systems, she exposed her cyber signature to a cybermenace. Every computer geek develops his or her own signature; it's sort of like every person has a unique set of fingerprints. So, when Annie went online at the computer lab at Littleton, and went deeper than any college geek can go, Hector had her. He recognized Annie's signature from the day before when she worked with DOA and me at Netti Barn, and he most likely backtracked her signature to two years ago. Before she left Littleton, Hector sent Annie the warning to back off. Hector isn't only after Joy and me, he's after Annie."

John addresses Fred, "Director Gaffney is sending some FBI backup. Until then, I need you and Steve to hunt Hector as well as you hunted Charles Eaton Alden."

Not even a toaster?

Before anyone moves, Kitt addresses John, "Why don't you and Joy just leave Mayflower? If Hector wants you two, if that's his endgame, won't he follow you and just leave the rest of us alone?"

Fred takes Kitt's hand in his and answers her question, "It's too late for that. Hector already knows that someone at Littleton College was working in the computer lab trying to find him. He probably already knows who that person is. If not, it won't be long before he knows it's Annie. Once he has her name, he'll find out where she lives, and he'll find her connection to John Maxwell, the owner of a software design company. Hector won't even have to work to figure anything out, he will have successfully unmasked Sam Sawyer. Everyone in this room, and Callie and Tess, are at risk. We can handle this, Kittridge, if we work together," Fred finishes with a wink. "Trust me."

Kitt looks at Fred, then at John, "I trust you, Fred."

Detective Fred Serpico leaves the living room, places two calls, then returns with the previously confiscated weapons. He hands them back to their rightful owners and lays out his plan. "First up, Annie needs to be taken out of the picture. I've arranged for her to stay at Officer Mike Monopoli's place. He will be Annie's 24-hour protection until Hector is caught or killed." He addresses Annie, "No school, no computers, no cell phones, no landline calls, no going out, no nothing. You do what Officer Monopoli says to do when he says to do it. Do you understand?"

Annie nods.

Fred goes at her again, "Annie, if you break any of those rules, you're not only putting yourself in danger, you'll be exposing the rest of us. But more to the point, you'll be jeopardizing your first line of defense, which is Mike."

Annie nods, "I won't do anything. I promise."

"Next up, Callie and Tess. Kitt, go pack some things for the girls while Annie packs her things." When everything is pulled together, Fred addresses Steve, "Take Annie to Monopoli's place. Then, get Maura, Callie, and Tess out of Mayflower. Take them to the place we talked about when we first became partners. Wait for me to contact you."

Before Steve and Annie leave, there is a knock at the kitchen door. Everyone, but Fred, pulls their gun and trains it at the man on the porch. The big bear of a man raises his hands, "White cops with guns—it's my personal nightmare. If you don't mind, I've already taken a hit this month."

Fred walks through the ring of potential fire and escorts the man into the room. "Sorry about that, Cluster. You damn fools, I called the sergeant and explained some of the situation and asked for his help. Now, if you would holster your weapons, I'm sure Cluster would appreciate it. I know I would. Okay Cluster, this is what I need you to do. You're still on desk duty at Littleton, right?"

Cluster grunts an unhappy response.

"Good. I need you at the security cameras, all day, every day, starting Monday morning. You know the faces and the routines of the Littleton people. I think the chance is low, but just in case a mid-thirty to mid-forty year-old FBI clone puts himself on campus, you'll be the first to know. I think the shit will hit the fan before then, but our suspect has his sights set on Littleton right now."

"Jane, and a couple of volunteers are at the college working on the Annual Fund mailing. I think I'll swing by and check on them. I'll take a look at the security footage from tonight."

Fred smacks Cluster on the shoulder, "Call if there's anything." He waits until the man leaves, then addresses the agents, "I've been thinking about what Annie said. I think she is dead-on about Hector being a FICA wannabe. This protracted search for the Boy Genius and the new game of *you kill me, or I kill you* wreaks of someone who's pissed at FICA." He turns to

Annie, "Leave the printouts of the computer searches and cross-referencing stuff you did at Littleton with Joy. She's the huntress, let's have her hunt. If you need to convey anything, tell Monopoli. He'll be using a burner. Don't touch that phone or any other electrical device."

"Not even a toaster?" Annie jokes.

"NO!" the room's occupants shout.

Fred pulls Annie in for a hug, "Be safe, Pixie."

Annie hugs everyone, even DOA.

Kitt follows her firstborn to the door, wraps her in her arms, and whispers, "I love you more than peanut butter."

Annie laughs, then tears at the reference. She said those words to her mom every day until the fourth grade, when she hit "the year of independence". Annie kisses her mother's cheek and leaves with Steve.

Kitt goes directly to her bedroom.

THE MENACE

Hector watches a little bit of a thing with long, honey-colored hair being escorted from an impressive bungalow at 22 Tarrington Way, Laurel Falls. When he pulled the thread left behind by the neophyte, it led to Annie Mahoney-Maxwell, a senior at Littleton College. He quickly learned that the student lives with her mother, Kitt Mahoney at this beachfront place. It took the cybermenace even less time to learn that the father of Annie is a software designer named, John Maxwell.

"Fucking John Maxwell? I had him on my list early on, but..." "You took him off," Troy laughs. "Why did you take him off the list?" "He didn't fit the profile of an agent. He's the owner and operator of a two-bit software design company called, Netti Barn. I had him do some design work for me, so I could check him out." "And..." "And his place is a small operation. It's just him and a couple of interns. There wasn't anything to suggest he was FBI or FICA." "What did you expect, a fucking sign? Looks like you fucked up, again, Hector." "Fuck you, Troy."

The menace keeps his eyes on the two people on the driveway. "Looks like Annie is leaving with an armed escort." Hector runs the license plates on the black Land Rover they get into. "Steve Phelps, an MFPD detective, is taking Annie Mahoney-Maxwell somewhere. Let's follow along and find out where they're heading." "Okay, but you'll have to drive," Troy laughs.

I hope you poisoned theirs.

Officer Monopoli closes his door after Detective Phelps leaves. "Make yourself at home, Annie. I think you know where everything is."

Annie hasn't been to Mike's condo, or even spoken to him since she crawled out of his bed the other night. The first guy Annie has ever thought about having sex with is the last guy who should be protecting her. But it is – what it is. Annie wants Mike; the problem is that they started a thing when she needed him. Annie Mahoney-Maxwell needs no one, so she is perplexed by her feelings for Mike, and she is pissed that she doesn't know how to separate her feelings of want and need for the young officer. She's not even sure why the distinction matters. All she knows for sure is that something is stopping her from being with Mike—but nothing is stopping her from lusting after him. How could she not? He is tall, dark, and handsome. Her mother, who describes all men by their NFL doppelganger says Mike is a dead ringer for New England Patriots, Danny Amendola. Annie likes that. And she likes Mike Monopoli.

Bullet Bungalow

John emails Director Gaffney a list of twenty names that Annie isolated as FICA wannabes. The list has last names and first initials only, so the group anticipates a wait for information. While they wait, Joy is doing a search based on Annie's work, and John is peering over her shoulder. She hates that on a good day—this is **not** a good day, so John moves on. Fred is at the stove finishing the last of six grilled cheese sandwiches. He plates two, grabs a wine glass and an open bottle of Moscato, and calls over his shoulder, "Help yourselves."

DC

"Maxwell made contact. He gave me a list of suspects to research. Hector's real name is on the list."

"What's the plan?"

"I'm going to give the fucker up. Then I'm going to make sure I get DOA into my hands."

"My hands."

"Yes."

Master Bedroom

Fred finds Kitt curled into a near fetal position on his side of the bed with Beatles tunes softly playing in the background. She is shrouded in near-darkness, rhythmic ocean sounds wafting through the open bedroom window. Fred turns on a table lamp, its soft, warm light falls gently across Kitt's tear-stained face. "The open window," he moves to close it, "not a good idea, right now, Kittridge. It wouldn't look too good if a seasoned detective and two super-spies let Hector breach security by coming through an open window."

Kitt chuckles as she unfurls herself.

Fred sits next to her on the bed. "By the way, we're switching pillows, tonight. You got mine all wet."

She chuckles again.

Fred holds out the plate of sandwiches and a glass of Moscato, "You need to eat some of this and drink some of this."

Kitt scooches into a sitting position and takes half a sandwich.

It isn't until she sits up that Fred sees that she's pulled her long hair high on her head in a messy up-do. Cascading ringlets frame her face and along the nape of her neck. Fred is taken aback by how drop dead gorgeous Kitt is. On their faux, faux, date, he remarked that she looks like Evangeline Lilly. But better. Now that they are together, he knows that Kitt Mahoney is as beautiful inside as she is outside. And she is *kick you in the ass beautiful* on the outside. He leans toward his woman, and places gentle kisses across her tear-touched lashes. He follows the path they have taken, finally finding her mouth. He kisses the corners of her lips, slowly working inward. His final kiss is whisper soft, chaste. "Trust me, Kittridge. I just found you, I'm not going to lose you, or anyone you love. I promise."

She kisses Fred long and deep.

After they eat, and share a glass of wine, Kitt gets up from the bed and heads toward her home office. She stands at the door waiting for Fred to follow her. He follows. She closes the door behind them. "Did you make sandwiches for them, too?"

He nods.

"I hope you poisoned theirs!"

He shakes his head.

"There's always next time. I'll do the cooking from now on. Don't worry Fred, I'll make sure you get the one that's okay to eat," she winks and grins, devilishly.

Fred shakes his head disapprovingly, "Really, Kittridge, you need to stop making death threats in my presence."

"Noted. Have you heard from Mike Monopoli yet?"

"No. We're on a four-hour call cycle. If I don't hear from him once in every four hours, then I'll know there's a problem."

"Oh," is all she says as she moves to a wall of framed artwork the kids gave her over the years. She takes a frame from the wall and hands it to Fred.

He looks at the picture. "What am I looking at, Kittridge?"

"A Mother's Day picture that Annie drew for me. It shows Netti Barn in the background, and John, Callie, Tess, Annie, and her favorite intern, Fee, in the foreground. Turn it over Fred; Annie put all their names on the back."

"Why am I looking at it, Kittridge?"

"Read the names, Fred."

"Dad, Callie, Tess, Annie, and Fee."

"Turn the picture over and look at the T-shirts Annie drew on each of them. Read the initials."

"D, C, T, A, J."

"The initials should be D, C, T, A, F, for Dad, Callie, Tess, Annie, and Fee," she reminds him.

"Wow, Kittridge. Do you think Annie knew way back then that Fee Peterson was Joy Ann Watts?"

"Not consciously. But…" Kitt's sentence is interrupted by a knock.

John is standing on the opposite side of the bedroom door when Fred opens it. He says two words, "Troy Ward."

The team assembles in the living room. The agents repeat what Director Gaffney pulled from the FICA files about an FBI wannabe named Troy Ward.

"Gaffney said that if our guy is a wannabe, then it's Ward," Joy begins. "He was in graduate school at MIT when Gaffney approached him.

He's a genius like John, but he's nuts—Gaffney's words not mine."

John gets into the conversation, "Based on skill level alone, Gaffney says Troy Ward and I are equals. Joy told me the other day that the only two defenders she can't defeat are Hector and me, which confirms Gaffney's assessment. He also just told us that Ward failed his first psych exam. It's FBI protocol that a second exam be given before a candidate is blackballed from consideration. Ward failed his second exam in an even bigger way than the first. Gaffney couldn't reveal the results, but I deduce that Troy Ward thinks he's..."

"Hector of Troy," Fred finishes John's sentence.

He nods and Joy jumps in, "When I was off the grid, I did research on hector, the word..."

"It means to bully or threaten someone, right?" Kitt interrupts.

"Yes, and it's fitting because Hector bullied me for two years, and now he's threatening me. After researching the word, I researched Hector from Greek and Roman mythology. In Homer's epic poem, *Iliad*, Hector was the greatest defender of Troy, and when he goes beyond the walls in search of his greatest rival, Achilles, he becomes the greatest hunter."

Fred's back in, "Sam Sawyer is the greatest defender, and DOA is the greatest hunter of cyberland. In order for Hector to ascend to their positions he needs to kill his greatest rivals."

John veers off the Hector/Troy analysis for a minute, "According to Gaffney, when Troy Ward failed his psych exam and lost out on the FICA defense position, he had a breakdown. He left MIT, never completed his PhD work, and was institutionalized on and off for years. That matches the pattern of his on and off search for me."

Joy jumps back in, "Hector is from Boston. He's gonna flip a nut when he learns that Sam Sawyer, aka John Maxwell, lives an hour away in Mayflower, and that DOA, aka Joy Ann Watts, just spent a month in Beantown."

"If Troy Ward is from Massachusetts, he's gonna know all about Littleton College. We should expect a visit from this nutcase anytime now," Fred adds.

THE MENACE

Hector, also known as Troy Ward, sits outside a condo complex in a sleepy corner of Mayflower. The sea-weathered wood and red brick building houses eight beachfront condos, some with corner to corner patios overlooking the Atlantic Ocean. He followed the detective and the student up Slater, and has been waiting twenty minutes to find out what comes next. He smiles when Detective Phelps comes out alone. "Well. Well. Annie Mahoney-Maxwell is staying with someone at Cutters. Don't know who you're with, Annie, but I will soon enough. First, I need to see what's next on the detective's agenda." "**We** need to see, Hector." "Shut up, Troy."

Hector follows the Land Rover to 2 Primrose Lane, a beautiful tree-lined street not too far from the condos. Detective Phelps enters a white two-story Victorian with a wide-planked wrap porch, and comes out within minutes with a smoking-hot Jessica Rabbit lookalike and two high school aged girls. Hector glances at his open laptop then back at the honey-haired teens. "Callie and Tess. John Maxwell has three daughters. I only need one—for now."

The Menace follows the Land Rover to I-495S before circling back to the beachfront condo. "Troy, the detective is taking the younger girls out of harm's way. "Good. Annie's the one we want, and there's no way she's getting out of harm's way. Neither is whoever's babysitting her." Hector parks in a visitor parking space, and walks up to the entrance. He engages the record option on his cell phone and reads aloud the eight names from the mail slots: "Henderson 1A, Sergeant 1B, Murphy 1C, Butler 1D, Monopoli 2A, Bodreau 2B, Sneade 2C, Buck 2D." Once back in his Civic, Hector grabs his laptop, taps in the residents' names, and gets to work. Within minutes, he knows where Annie is staying, "She's with Officer Michael Monopoli, at 2A."

"Sleep well, Annie. Tomorrow's gonna be a long day," they say.

Didn't see that coming.

Fred, Joy, and John are in the kitchen doing "things". The detective is fielding check-in calls and pulling Officer Speil onto the case. Joy is keystroking the hell out of Troy Ward aka Hector. John is full-out pacing the bungalow. This circumstance is particularly worrisome because John does not pace. But – he – is – pacing. When he cuts through the kitchen on his way from the porch to the living room, Fred informs, "Steve arrived at his destination with Maura, Callie, and Tess. If this shit goes sideways, John, I left Steve's location in my safe in Kitt's room."

John nods.

Fred continues. "Officer Monopoli, reported that Annie is safe and settled in for the night. Speil is gonna stop by Mike's in the morning to put another set of eyes on Annie, until then, he's gonna drive by Cutters, Netti, and Bullet Bungalow."

All activity stops when Kitt enters the kitchen. "Fred, what are the plans for tonight?"

"We'll all stay here until there's some movement. Why?"

"John and Joy will need a place to sleep and freshen up. John, why don't you take Annie's room? Joy, why don't you take Tess' room? It's the one with pink and white chevron wallpaper at the top of the stairs." Kitt is met with stunned silence—she ignores it and continues, "Joy, I won't know if you go through Tess' belongings, but she will. So, just put back anything you look at." Kitt walks to Joy and hands her some things, "You can change into these, if you want. There's a shower upstairs. Oh, and Joy, you should look at Tess' things. Get to know her. She's a great kid." With that, Kitt says goodnight and goes back to her bedroom.

"Didn't see that coming," a detective and two super-spies say in unison.

A Daughter's Room

Joy stands in the doorway for many minutes with Kitt's words tumbling through her head, and tripping from her lips, "Get to know her. She's a great kid." When the mother's rapidly beating heart gets back to a normal thump, she enters the pink and white chevron papered room. "Get to know her. Well, the paper speaks volumes," she laughs. She puts her things just inside the door, and makes her way to the window for a reverse view. She likes what she sees, "It's lived in, but cared for." She goes to a tallboy chest of drawers on the far wall, behind which is a framed grouping of headshots, "Grade school pictures." Her heart picks up that thumping beat again. "She was adorable. Fresh faced, and squeaky clean, pigtail braids, and missing teeth. And those big, blue eyes, and that…" Joy leans in, her fingertips automatically raising to touch a tiny, teardrop dimple under her daughter's eye, "She has my dimple. I forgot that she has my dimple."

The birthmother sits on the edge of her daughter's bed, and takes a minute. It's the amount of time she will allow herself—one minute to wonder what her life would have been like had she had a family when she was growing up, if she'd had a place to call "home" if she had stayed and created a family with John, rather than creating a life and walking away from it. "Water under the bridge, Joy."

She gets up and continues her tour of the 14-year-old girl's room. She starts at a coatrack that is chuck full of jackets, and backpacks, and duffle bags, and sweatshirts. She takes one off a hook, "This is her favorite, or at least it's the one she most often wears when she goes to school." Joy holds it, smells it, hugs it—puts it on. She admires her view in a press-on mirror on the inside of the closet door. The small woman with cropped blonde hair, and piercing blue eyes gets lost in the orange garment with black MFRHS lettering, and black tiger on the chest. Its sleeves hang below her fingertips, the waistband hits her hip—it is a size too big and, "It's perfect."

Joy is pulled toward the teenager's desk, and as she moves towards it she repeats Kitt's earlier warning, "I won't know if you go through Tess' belongings, but she will. So, just put back anything you look at." The super-spy, the ghost, smirks knowing that she could go through the entire room without so much as disturbing a speck of dust. Joy sits, Joy searches, Joy hits paydirt. She reaches into the bottom left hand drawer, "Journals." The ones on the bottom, clearly the oldest of the group have cartoon characters, and block ABCs, and happy little garden scenes on their covers. Joy takes the oldest one from the stack, and cracks it open. It's mostly filled with very young penmanship, Tess' name written over and over, and Callie's, too. Simple drawings with simple words tell a story—the beginnings of a life's recording. Joy puts it back and takes the top journal, the one with a pink and white chevron cover. "Tess sure does like the up and down pattern. I wonder if that's significant." When she cracks the spine on this one, she sees the penmanship of a teenaged girl, reads the words of an introspective young woman.

> *Dear Diary,*
>
> *It happened again. Callie and I started school today, and everyone said that we look like twins. We do. Anyone who looks can see that we are sisters. Anyone who listens knows that we are only sort of sisters. Mrs. McTigue, our homeroom teacher took attendance—that's always when people learn that we aren't real sisters, not like Annie and Callie are real sisters. "Callie Mahoney-Maxwell," Mrs. McTigue called out.*

"Here," Callie answered. "Tess Maxwell," the teacher called out. "Here," I replied.

Joy got pissed. Joy got sad. Joy got really pissed. "See. No matter how loved a kid is, there is always a hole that never gets filled." She puts Tess' things back, and puts the blame for her daughter's hurt feelings where it belongs—on her. She tidies up from her tour, nestles into a corner, pulls her gear near, and goes deep—it's where she belongs—the only place where she feels whole—at least it was—before she stepped into the pink and white chevron papered bedroom of a 14-year-old girl named, Tess Maxwell.

Cutters Cove
Mike takes Annie's things to his bedroom.

"Really Mike, I don't mind sleeping on the couch."

"I'd mind, Annie. Besides, I don't want you anywhere near the front door." He puts her bags on the bed and turns to leave. She takes hold of his hand, not sure what his reaction will be. He wraps his fingers through hers and looks into her gold-flecked, acorn-brown eyes. They tell of her thoughts.

"You don't need to say anything, Annie. When you figure out the whole want thing versus need thing, I'll still be here." Mike brushes her long hair off her shoulders and gently plays with the silky strands. Then he pulls her tight against him and kisses her, "Goodnight, Sweet Annie."

Fred, I need to tell.

John is up early, and putting on a pot of coffee when Kitt enters the kitchen. She freezes, then starts to turn away.
"Can we talk?"
"You hurt me, John."
"I know. Can we talk about it?"
"I'll try."
He grabs their Mom and Dad mugs from the cupboard and fills them. They quietly sit opposite one another for many minutes. Kitt's body-language whispers that she is surrendering some of her anger and disappointment. John's body-language has gone mute. Not a single word is spoken between them. Really, what can be said?

Mayflower-Falls Regional Medical Center
Sergeant David Cluster, enters the hospital at 6:30 AM for his physical therapy session. When Detective Serpico asked him for help, the security officer asked his therapist if they could move his session up a day. He could, so Cluster is feeling good from his workout, and smelling good from his shower. "I think I might just surprise Miss Jane Harper of Savannah, Georgia, with a bite of breakfast Cluster," he laughs, then jumps into his Jeep and heads to

Slater—the musical score from *Gone with the Wind* humming on his lips.

Cutters

Mike shifts beneath Annie, trying hard not to disturb her. Given his current predicament, something very hard may very well disturb her. Annie snuggles against him. She joined him on the couch in the wee hours of the morning, "For just a minute," she said, before falling into a deep sleep sprawled across his chest. He brushes Annie's bangs aside and stares at her face, her beautiful face. A little pixie with big expressive eyes, Mike marvels at how much she looks like Ariana Grande. But better.

Annie shifts again and nuzzles deep. She feels something hard pressed against her hip, reaches down to move whatever it is, and jumps off when she realizes what she's touched. "Oh, Mike, I'm so sorry. I didn't mean to...I mean I didn't expect to...I mean, I've got to go."

Mike reaches out and takes hold of Annie's hand, trying hard not to laugh. "You can't go. Come here, Annie." He pulls her back on top of him, "Let's start this day over."

Annie stretches out on top of the man who held her close all night. He wraps his arms around her then rolls her beneath him. He presses Annie deep into the couch. She whispers against his cheek, "Mike, I want you and I need you."

Mike kisses Annie the way he's wanted to for weeks, "You've got me, Annie."

Slater

Officer Speil drove by Monopoli's place and Netti Barn three times each since Detective Serpico pulled him onto the case. He's back at Cutters Cove parking lot and going into the condo building to check on Mike and Annie. He owes the detective a four-hour check-in call, but he decides to make it from Mike's condo. Speil parks next to an empty Honda Civic that's been at Cutters all night. He grabs the tray of Perks coffees and pumpkin chai tea he picked up on the way, and starts toward the door. He makes it to the landing and presses the buzzer for 2A, right before everything goes dark. He thinks he hears someone say, "Welcome back, Officer Speil," before he hits the ground.

Mike groans at the sound of his door buzzer, "Damn it. That'll be Speil. We were going to the gym this morning, but Fred put him on the case last night. He's checking up on us."

"Get off! Get off! Oh my God, Mike, get off!" Annie yells.

He laughs as he pulls Annie up with him. He presses the button for the downstairs entry and watches as Annie scurries out of the room.

"Wait, wait Mike. Okay, you can open the door," Annie calls from his bedroom.

Mike opens the door, then tries to slam it shut when he sees the gun.

Annie never heard the shot; it was silenced. Annie never heard Mike hit the floor; Hector cushioned his fall. Annie never knew she was in danger, until Hector put a chloroform cloth over her face.

Bullet Bungalow

Fred is pissed. Speil missed his four-hour check-in. Fred is worried. Monopoli missed his four-hour check-in. Fred is just about to call for a cruiser to do a check at Monopoli's when his phone rings. He sees it's Cluster. "I'm busy, Cluster," he growls into the phone.

"Serpico! Listen! I was on my way back from Mayflower-Falls Regional, traveling down Slater."

Slater is where Monopoli lives. Fred braces for the bad news.

"Detective, I almost hit a guy stumbling in the street. It's Speil. I get him in my car, and he starts mumbling about Mike and Annie, so I go to check on them. Mike's been shot. Annie's gone. The ambulance just arrived, but Mike's out of it. It's bad."

Detective Serpico disconnects from Cluster. "Everyone, kitchen NOW!" he shouts.

Kitt and John arrive immediately. Joy arrives a minute later.

"Speil's injured. Monopoli's shot. Annie's gone!"

Before Fred can say another word, John's cell phone rings with an alert, "Netti Barn's been breached. It's got to be Hector. Come on, Fred. Joy, you stay with Kitt." The men are running toward the door when Joy grabs hold of Fred's arm. "Fred, I need to tell…"

"Come on Serpico!" John yells.

Kitt runs to her bedroom. She returns almost immediately dressed in jeans and a sweatshirt. She looks at Joy, "Are you coming?"

"We're staying, here, Kitt."

The mother of a kidnap victim grabs her car keys from a hook by the back door.

"Kitt, I can't let you leave!"

"Are you going to shoot me, Joy?" Kitt asks pointedly.

"If I have to."

"Well then, you're going to have to." With that, Kitt turns and walks out the back door.

Joy follows.

He just shoots the fucker.

"Hector, you messed up!" "No, Troy, you messed up!"

Annie lays quietly on the floor of Netti Barn, suffering the lingering effects of chloroform. She plays as though she is still unconscious. *I need to buy time.* She knows the alarms at Netti Barn have been triggered. *Dad will get the signal on his cell. Dad and Fred, will come.*

"We shouldn't have taken her, Troy? I want John Maxwell, not this cyber huntress wannabe." "Maxwell will come for her, Hector. He will trade his life for hers," the madman paces back and forth occasionally glancing at Annie. His internal fight is spewing out of control. "This isn't the way this is supposed to go down, Troy. You messed up, again! Just like you did on the FICA psych exam. I got the Director interested in my computer skills, and you went all batshit crazy during the interviews and exams. I could have been the Boy Genius of FICA. I **am** the Boy Genius of cyberland." "You're **nothing** without me, Hector! You can't survive in the real world like me. You need to be in cyberland, spending all your time hunting. With what? Keystrokes! You can't kill the super-spies of FICA with keystrokes. You need one of these." Troy Ward waves an AK-47 and fires off a few rounds, "You take care of cyberland, Hector. I'll take care of the FICA defender and huntress when they come for her."

A tremble takes hold of Annie. She is starting to lose whatever control she still has. A mantra tumbles on a whisper, "Dad. Fred. Please come. Dad. Fred. Please come. Dad..." The repeated droning of those words and the effects of the chloroform brings fatigue back upon her. She is surrendering to sleep's protective pull when a growing sense of dread hits her—**hard**. "Mike." Tears fill Annie's eyes as she remembers that Mike was her protection. "He wouldn't let anyone take me. He would have protected me with his life." Annie's whispered acknowledgement breaks her heart. She closes her eyes tight—opens them when she feels a subtle change in the air. "Dad. Fred. You've come," she whispers the prayer of thanks.

A police bullhorn blares, "Troy Ward. This is the Mayflower-Falls Police Department. We have the building surrounded. Come out with your hands up."

"See, Troy. You messed up! I'm never gonna be the Boy Genius at FICA!" "Shut the hell up, Hector! I'm in control now!"

Annie feels a dramatic change in the madman's words. They become snarling. Otherworldly. Troy drags her to her feet and pulls her tight against him. Terror seizes her.

Memories of Charles Eaton Alden pulling her to his chest and assaulting her at Littleton College surge from wherever they've been hiding and crash against this moment with Troy. Her senses flood. Annie goes limp against her captor. He lifts her over his shoulder and carries her to the loft.

Fred and John make it into Netti Barn during the bullhorn announcement. They move silently toward the far walls, taking position on opposite sides of the massive room. The ramblings of a madman echo around them, allowing their movements to go unnoticed. They position themselves at the bottom of twin sets of stairs that lead to the loft.

Troy drops Annie to the floor, grabs her by her hair, and drags her across the loft. "Don't move," he snarls. He pushes open a massive window, grabs her to a standing position and presses her between him and the window frame. He holds his assault rifle high for all to see. The madman looks out at the gathering below. It is a scene he imagined he'd be part of a million times. Of course, he never imagined he'd be on this side of the event, being hunted as a criminal. He takes in the scene again. Cops, ambulances, fire trucks as far as the eye can see, all waiting for their call to action. A few spectators have been cordoned off, but in amongst the emergency personnel, Troy spots two women. One has long brown hair, and the other has short blonde hair. He knows one of them is DOA, "Troy, that's DOA." "Who's DOA?" Troy demands as he wedges Annie between him and the window.

"What?" Annie asks completely confused by the back and forth talking madman.

"There, those two women. Which one is DOA?"

Annie looks to where her captor is looking. She sees her mom and Joy. She shakes her head and remains silent.

"Fine, have it your way. I'll take them both out."

Joy trains her eyes on the loft window and watches as the madman surveys the scene. He has Annie wedged tight between him and the window. "He's focused on the outside. That means that he doesn't know John and Fred are inside. They have a chance. What's he doing? What's he looking for?" A flicker from the window pulls Joy's attention, clarifies the moment. It all happens in a split second—she sees Hector position his rifle—she jumps in front of Kitt, shielding her from Hector's bullet. The women hit the ground wrapped in each other's arms.

Fred and John burst into the loft from two different directions when they hear the shot.

Annie slips from Hector's grasp when he moves from the window. She begins crab-walking away from the madman. He reaches and grabs hold of her leg.

John shoots the fucker. He doesn't try to engage him.

HE JUST SHOOTS THE FUCKER.

Fred races to Hector, kicks his dropped weapon away, and checks for a pulse. "He's alive, but not for long."

John races to Annie and pulls her tight. He hears her whisper.

"Hector shot them." She points to the window.

He settles her onto a couch, and moves to the loft window. When he looks out, he sees the only two women he has ever loved sprawled on the ground. One is being worked on by paramedics. The other is holding the fallen woman's hand and sobbing.

Her condition is critical.

Hector is dead before paramedics make it to the loft. Joy Ann Watts is barely alive when the ambulance she's in speeds away from Netti. When John arrives at Mayflower-Falls Regional, he is met outside Emergency by an FBI agent.

"Special Agent Maxwell, my name is Agent Dan Shea. I am part of a field team that was dispatched by Director Gaffney to Netti Barn this morning; part of that team is a medical unit. Special Agent Watts was transported by members of the FBI and remains under guard in the operating room."

"Her condition?"

"Critical, sir. I will keep you apprised of her condition."

The emergency room corridors quickly fill with friends and coworkers of Kitt and Annie. John recognizes many of them from the night he stood vigil for Cluster. There are others assembled now, most of them are from the MFPD. That's because there are two people fighting for their lives after being shot by a madman known as Hector: Joy Ann Watts and Michael Monopoli. John hasn't moved from the spot outside Emergency when an ambulance arrives with Kitt and Annie.

"Dad," Annie begins to cry when she sees him. She reaches out and takes hold of his hand as the gurney passes, quickly losing it as the EMTs maneuver her through a set of sliding doors and down the corridors toward an exam room.

"Coming through," someone shouts from over his shoulder. He turns to see Kitt's gurney that's out of the ambulance and on the move. He steps back as she is wheeled past and into the same room as their daughter. He is left outside in the ambulance bay with Fred who slaps his shoulder—the universal "guys" show of support.

"Nice shot, John. I particularly liked the *fucker* comment."

"Said that out loud, did I?"

"Twice. Any news on Joy?"

"She's in the OR. Her condition is critical." John gets another slap to his shoulder as Fred steps into the ER. The father remains outside until the daughter returns from X-ray. The kidnap victim has the all-clear on her previously fractured wrist, but is wearing an immobilization glove and a sling, and she is suffering effects of chloroform which has left her with a pounding headache. Mostly, though, the young woman is suffering from a near broken heart. Officer Grant Speil, who is sporting a line of stitches just above his ear, courtesy of Hector knocking him out cold, greets Annie with soft words.

"He's fighting, Annie. Believe me, he's gonna do everything he can to come back to you."

John's daughter falls into the officer's arms and sobs. When she pulls away, she takes hold of his hand and lets him lead her to the surgical unit. Before they have reached the elevators, they are met by David Cluster and Jane Harper. The four of them exchange long hugs, and whispered words, then head up to stand in hope for Mike. Kitt returns from having a CT-scan with the all-clear on a concussion. She, too, is sporting a sling to help with a shoulder injury and is bearing the effects of hitting her head during Joy's tackle.

"John." She finds and holds his eyes. "Joy..." she says as her eyes fill.

John walks to her and takes her into his arms. "She's fighting," he says, although he doesn't know that to be true. Admittedly, he doesn't know anything. "What happened?"

Kitt shakes her head, "I'm not sure exactly. Hector wedged Annie against the window. Joy mumbled a few things about you and Fred being inside, then there was a shiny flash coming from the loft, and before I knew it, Joy tackled me, and we hit the ground. She was mostly on top of me, and when I tried to get out from under her, my hands got covered in...and Joy started mumbling...and..."

John pulls Kitt back into his arms, kisses her temple, and lets her cry a bit, then he lets her go to the man who is eager to hold her.

"I'm heading up to the surgical unit," John says to no one, really. When he gets there, he finds Annie and Grant sitting in face to face chairs, knees touching and hands holding. The Mahoney-Maxwell clan has never been a church-going family, but Annie is clearly in prayer for the young officer. John stops and offers a prayer of his own, although he can't imagine that his words will cut through the many layers of his misdeeds. Nonetheless, he is called to try.

"Is there a Detective Fred Serpico here?" a nurse in surgical scrubs asks just as Fred, Kitt, Steve, and Maura exit an elevator.

"I'm Detective Serpico," he says, as he approaches the nurse.

"I have your name as contact person for Officer Michael Monopoli."

The floor goes quiet. John sees Annie drop her head into her hands. Grant places one of his gently on top of her head—maybe for her—maybe for him.

"Detective, Officer Monopoli made it through surgery. He is in critical condition in the Surgical ICU. If you have contact information for his next of kin, you should be in touch with them." The nurse places a hand to Fred's forearm and gives it a gentle squeeze, "I will be out to update you every hour."

Maura intercepts the surgical nurse. They exchange a few words and share a few head shakes and a hug. John's daughter chooses that moment to lift her teary eyes upward. She puts her head back into hands that fall to her knees.

John follows Maura to Kitt, Fred, and Steve, to hear the truth.

An ashen Maura gives them the truth. "The bullet fractured Mike's shoulder joint causing extensive muscle and bone damage. He nearly bled out from a nicked artery. There were complications during the surgical procedure. It's touch and go. What about Mike's family, Fred?"

"They live in Italy. Mike came here for college and never went back. I'll call them in the morning, their time. Maybe we'll know something more by then."

"John," Kitt pulls his focus after a few minutes of nothingness. "We need to decide what we are going to do."

He stares blankly.

"About Tess and Joy," she says, then turns when Maura gasps at the sight of the surgical nurse returning...

He just walks away.

Out of the corner of his eye, John catches sight of the FBI agent who stopped him outside Emergency when he first arrived. The agent begins walking toward John, his head shaking back and forth, already signaling the news he's about to deliver.

John's heart thumps an erratic beat
because he knows—
Joy is gone.

The End

More to come …

Please enjoy the teaser for my next book in the series,
Cutters Cove …

Cutters Cove

THE CARTEL

--- PULLING THREADS ---

Book Three

SHERYLL O'BRIEN

I hardly knew ye.
October

Fred gave Kitt's hand a gentle squeeze. She gave him a "deer caught in the highlights" look. She stepped to the casket of Joy Ann Watts and placed a single white rose onto the pale birch box. The perfect bud was beautifully tied with hand-embroidered ribbon that had been passed down through generations of Mahoney women. The Mahoney woman present that day chose a white rose and the white ribbon because...

Kitt took a moment for private reflection, then walked to the head of the casket and looked at the tiny group of mourners. The only people present that day were family and friends of Kitt, and yet it felt as though she was standing at Carnegie Hall in front of thousands of strangers, people who had gathered for a performance, for her performance. Kittridge Anne Mahoney was not at Carnegie Hall, she was at a centuries-old cemetery in Laurel Falls, Massachusetts, at the end of a barely paved lane, atop a tiny hill, at the freshly dug grave of a woman she barely knew—and didn't like all that much. Her role that day should have been nothing more than an attendee at the graveside service of Joy Ann Watts, and yet, there she was, at the head of the woman's casket readying herself to say a few words.

"There is very little that I know about Joy Ann Watts. I don't know what her favorite flower was or what her favorite color was. I don't know what her early years were like, or why she came to the choices she made in adulthood. I don't know if she was religious, or if she was guided by a higher spirit—but I do know this…

"Joy Ann Watts made sacrifices for the people she loved, and the nation she served. She put the wellbeing of others above her own, expected nothing in return, and shouldered her burdens in solitude. She did the right thing, even when it was the most difficult thing to do." Kitt let an unexpected wave of loss and grief settle, then found the face of a teenage girl standing graveside. She offered a tiny smile, in lieu of the hug she wanted to give her. She received nothing in return, so…

"The thought that I hold closest to my heart today, the thing that I believe most in my soul is this— Joy Ann Watts should have had the chance to know her daughter. Tess Maxwell should have had the chance to know her mother." Kitt took a step away then stopped. "I wish I had the chance to know Tess' mother, too."

ABOUT THE AUTHOR

She is not dead.

Sheryll O'Brien crafts characters without constraints. She tells them who they are, then let's them show her better versions of themselves. She gives them life and they live it beyond her wildest dreams.

Sheryll is a lifelong resident of Worcester, Massachusetts, where she is wife to the most supportive husband ever, and mother of two adult daughters, one who refuses to leave her home and the other who refuses to tell her where she lives. Of most significance, she is MammyGrams to the sweetest six-year-old, Hadley.

Sheryll worked several years in the fundraising community of Worcester County, writing grants for non-profit organizations. She began writing for her own pleasure after surviving brain surgery and breast cancer. Happily, for her fanbase of family and friends—she is not dead.

If you have enjoyed reading my book, I would very much appreciate you taking a few minutes to write a review and post that review on amazon.com and goodreads.com.

The opinion of readers can help prospective readers make a purchasing decision.

To learn more, please visit my website, www.pullingthreadsnovella.com
and subscribe to my blog for updates on future projects.

I would absolutely love to hear from my readers, you may email me at,

pullingthreadsnovella@gmail.com

www.ingramcontent.com/pod-product-compliance
Lightning Source LLC
Chambersburg PA
CBHW07082718O626
46818CB00001B/417